BOOK FOUR

MINDSPACE

ENDGAME

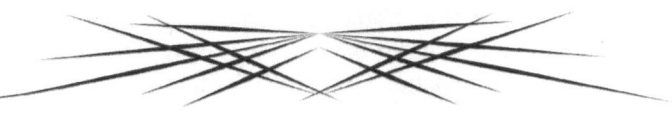

A K DUBOFF

Published by Dawnrunner Press
Cover Copyright © 2021 A.K. DuBoff

ISBN-10: 1954344147
ISBN-13: 978-1954344143
Copyright Registration Number: TX0008730706

0 9 8 7 6 5 4 3

Produced in the United States of America

TABLE OF CONTENTS

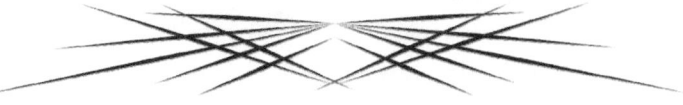

KEY TERMS, CAST & LOCATIONS

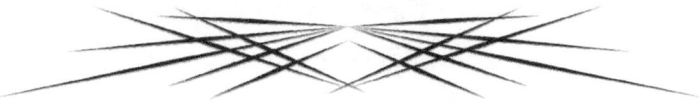

KEY TERMS

Taran – The race of all people in the Taran Empire; synonymous with human

Tararian Guard – The primary military force for the Taran Empire

Jump – Faster-than-light travel through subspace

Beacon Network – The navigation method for subspace jumps, maintained by SiNavTech

High Dynasties – The seven ruling families of the Taran Empire, collectively a governing council

Tararian Selective Service (TSS) – A quasi-military organization specializing in telekinesis; a complement to the Tararian Guard

Telepathic Receptor (TR) – An artificial neural structure composed of the mineral valteron; makes an individual susceptible to remote telepathic control

Priesthood – The former governing body of the Taran Empire

CAST

Tararian Guard

Kira Elsar – Captain, team leader

Ari Lanmore – Lance corporal, weapons specialist on Kira's team

Kyle Asher – Lance corporal, technical specialist on Kira's team

Nia Boro – Lance corporal, technical specialist on Kira's team

Lucas Sandren – Major, Kira's commanding officer

Terence Kaen – Colonel, Kira's chain-of-command (formerly possessed by an alien presence known as 'Nox')

Leon Caletti – Civilian consultant, geneticist/scientist, Kira's significant other

Jack – Technical specialist in Leon's lab

Tess – Technical specialist in Leon's lab

Deanna Olvera – Major, Orion Station head of security

Doctor Elric – Lead medical doctor for Orion Station base

Allen Lucian – General, leader of Orion Station base

Crew of the *Raven*

Rodrick – Captain
Aleya – First Officer
Sven – Support systems engineer
Gil – Mechanic

Elusian Alliance *(member world of Taran Empire)*

Elton Joris – President

Ellen Caletti – Press Secretary, former Mysaran spy (Leon's sister)
Nico – Assistant to President Joris

Mysaran Coalition *(independent world)*

Trisha Mercer – Mysaran political liaison for Ellen Caletti on Mysar

Fiona Wyles– Mysaran government administrator, and former 'enforcer' for Chancellor Hale

Cynthia Hale – Former Mysaran chancellor (deceased, formerly possessed by an alien presence known as 'Reya')

MTech *(Research company based on Mysar; branch on Valta)*

Monica Waylon – Director of MTech's lab on Valta (deceased)

Jared Frey – Monica's research assistant at the MTech lab (formerly possessed by an alien presence known as 'Nox')

LOCATIONS

Orion Station – Tararian Guard base

Elvar Trinary – Kira's home system (planets: Mysar, Valta, Elusia)

Gaelon System — Supposedly uninhabited star system adjacent to the Elvar Trinary

Tararia – The central planet of the Taran Empire

CHAPTER 1

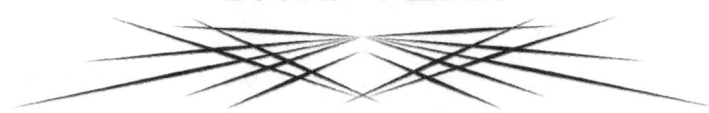

CAPTAIN KIRA ELSAR peeked out of the Protheon office door into the hallway. There were still no signs of security reinforcements.

"Sorry, Dave," she said to the poor sap bound in stasis cuffs on the office's floor. "Looks like your buddies are still out for lunch."

He muttered something through his gag. Though the words were unintelligible, the profound displeasure in his tone came through just fine—not surprising, given that he was getting acquainted with the flavor of his sock.

"I told you we wouldn't do anything if you cooperated and kept your mouth shut," Kira replied to his mutterings. "You *had* to keep talking."

"Dude should be thanking you for not going all mind-control on him," Kyle said while he worked at the terminal next to Nia.

Dave's eyes widened.

"Yeah, that's right, buddy," Kira said, casting what she

hoped was a menacing glare. "I could make you dance to whatever tune I wanted to play, if you force my hand. Just stay nice and quiet while we finish our work."

The bound security officer remained motionless and silent on the floor.

Kira nodded with satisfaction. "That's more like it, thank you."

<My, you're in a mood today!> Jasmine interjected in Kira's mind.

<You heard him! No one makes fun of my red hair,> she replied to the AI.

<I feel sorry for anyone who tries. You were across the room and had him on the floor faster than I've ever seen you move.>

<I'm finally getting the hang of directing these new nanites. May as well put them to good use.>

Jasmine made her equivalent of a sigh. *<Right, that's the* best *possible use for those abilities.>*

<Hey, gotta start somewhere!>

Compared to some of their ops, the mission had thus far gone according to plan. Dressed in office attire with light armor underneath, her team was meant to blend in with the other workers, accomplish their task, and then leave before anyone was the wiser. Dave's presence had been an unforeseen complication when they reached the datacenter control office deep within the facility. However, one underpaid, untrained sentry didn't stand a chance against *one* of the Guard soldiers, let alone Kira's team of four.

While Kira recognized that Dave was just doing his job, and she'd likely been harder on him than necessary, she couldn't help being on edge. It'd been calm in the month since the incident in Gaelon with the Trols. When things seemed to be going well, it almost certainly meant a crisis was right around the corner.

"I'm almost in," Kyle reported, looking over the information displayed on the eight monitors mounted above a glass desk along the wall opposite the door.

"These encryptions are deceptively tricky," Nia commented from the terminal next to him. She tugged at the neck of the blouse under her pantsuit.

"One of these days, we'll come across something that challenges you," Kira said.

"Can't wait." Kyle glanced over his shoulder at her. "And we're in."

"Good work." Kira approached his computer station while Ari took over covering the door. "So, what are we dealing with?" she asked.

"Shockingly, not all of the company's dealings have been as above-board as they'd like us to believe." Nia scanned over the information displayed on the main screen.

It was exactly the information they'd come to retrieve— financial transaction records, cargo logs, personnel assignments. There was no way Protheon would be able to deny smuggling charges with the Guard having that information in hand.

Kira crossed her arms. "Are there any corporations that *aren't* up to no good?"

Kyle began transferring the data to an external drive. "Few and far between, that's for sure."

"We've got company," Ari whispered from the doorway. He readied his multi-handgun on the sonic stun setting.

"*Of course* we do." Kira sighed.

Her team wasn't supposed to be in the Protheon corporate headquarters, and it was critical that no one trace the infiltration back to the Tararian Guard. Dave could say whatever he wanted, but there was nothing to connect Kira's team to the Taran military. If too many people showed up and started asking questions, though, it would become exponentially more difficult to hide the reason for the intrusion.

"Transfer is complete," Kyle stated from the terminal. He disconnected the external drive.

Kira pulled her multi-handgun from the satchel that was part of her disguise as a business professional. She tucked the weapon in the back waistband of her pants, under her blazer. "Make sure your digital tracks are covered," she told Kyle and Nia while moving toward to door. "I'll see if I can get rid of the visitor."

Ari stepped aside. "Good luck."

Kira nodded, then peeked outside to see what they were up against.

A frazzled-looking businessman was marching down the hall in their direction, a frown painted on his face and a tablet clutched in his hand.

<Jasmine, do you have anything on this guy?>

<Mark Elmer, middle manager in the Shipping division. I don't see anything on his calendar to explain his presence in this part of the building,> the AI replied.

<Maybe he'll go right past us,> Kira suggested. *<If we close the door and are quiet—>*

"Who would be accessing those files?" Mark muttered while consulting his tablet.

<Great, there goes that theory.> Kira composed her face in a pleasant smile, then ducked out from the communications room and closed the door behind her.

"Oh, hey, Mark! Nice to see you again," she greeted him with a wave.

The man stopped in his tracks. He gave her the once-over of someone trying to place a face with a name. "Uh, hi. Haven't seen you for a while," he replied after a pause. "Do you... work over here?"

"Just consulting on some projects," Kira replied. *<How do I get rid of this guy?>* she asked Jasmine.

<I thought that's what you were doing!>

<Well, fok.> She smiled. "I think I heard something about pizza in the lunch room."

<Kira, is this seriously your plan?> Jasmine did not sound amused or the least bit confident.

<Food is a great motivator! If I can distract him...>

"I'm vegan," Mark replied.

<Shite. Is there vegan pizza?>

<Kira! This isn't working.>

It was time for a different tactic.

"Are you here about the security notice?" Kira asked, shifting gears.

Mark frowned. "Yes. You got it, too?"

She took a step toward him and dropped her voice. "Look, I'm not even 'officially' working on this project, but I said I'd keep an eye on this while—"

<Jasmine, who's a higher-up mentioned in those files we just pulled? Someone who may be busy with other things.>

<Darlene is on vacation until the end of the week, according to the Out of Office notice on her email.>

"—Darlene is out of town," Kira continued out loud. "I was hoping to take care of this quietly. I don't want her to lose faith in me. I really need this job." She bit her lip and tried to look meek.

<You don't do 'helpless' well,> Jasmine commented.

<Yeah, well, if it works to get rid of this guy without me

having to mind-control him or bash his face in, it's worth a shot.>

Mark's scowl deepened. "What did you say your name was? I can't recall if we've met."

<That was a fail.> Kira slipped her right hand behind her back. "Shelly. I'm new." Internally, she continued her conversation with Jasmine. *<Is it possible for you to trigger the facility's fire alarm?>*

<Yes, I'm connected to the system. But I feel the need to remind you that our instructions were to keep a low profile.>

<It's a little late for that. Our best chance is a major distraction.>

"I'd like to see your credentials," Mark requested.

Kira patted her chest and hip with her left hand. "Darn, I think I left my badge at my desk."

<Would you like that alarm now?>

<Yes, please!>

A blaring siren erupted in the hall, causing Mark to jump. "What the…?" He looked up at the flashing red light.

"Oh shite!" Kira exclaimed. "Are they here? Darlene warned me…"

"Who?" Mark asked, clearly perplexed.

"She didn't tell you?" Kira swore under her breath. "Look, there's no time to explain. You have to check on the backups. We can't be found here."

Mark glanced in the direction he'd come from. "Shite. All right."

"Good luck." Kira acted like she was going to hurry away in the other direction. She took several steps, then glanced over her shoulder to make sure Mark was leaving.

When he turned a corner, Kira headed back to the office where her team was hiding out.

<Huh. That was either some smooth talking or that guy isn't

the brightest,> Jasmine said.

Kira smirked. *<Generic phrases let people autocomplete the thoughts with their worst fears. In the absence of food motivators, it's an old standby.>*

<Except with this alarm, security is going to be on high alert. I don't think you'll be able to talk us out of the rest of this.>

<Don't worry, I have a plan.>

Kira was certain Jasmine wasn't going to like that plan, so she decided to keep the details to herself for the time being.

As soon as she opened the office door, she was greeted by three handguns pointed in her direction.

Her team lowered the weapons when they saw it was her.

"What the fok did you do?" Ari asked in a low voice.

"I improvised." Kira turned her attention to Dave on the floor. "Sorry, buddy, looks like we're going to have to shoot you after all." She readied her multi-handgun. Her team quickly cleared the blast zone.

She fired a sonic blast, and Dave's head lolled to the side as he fell unconscious.

Nia raised an eyebrow. "Care to explain?"

"No easier way to clear a path than by posing as the heroes trying to help the injured guy," Kira replied with a mischievous grin.

Ari sighed. "I'll get his arms."

Kyle groaned. "Sandren is going to give us so much shite about this."

"Relax, everything is under control." Kira returned her handgun to the back of her waistband. "Follow my lead."

She stepped back into the hall. *<What's our optimized route to get out of here?>*

<One hundred meters to the left, then take a right, go down the 'D' stairwell to the ground floor. You should be able to slip

out with the other evacuees,> Jasmine replied.

<Perfect.> Kira nodded. "This way," she told her team.

Ari and Nia followed behind her, carrying unconscious Dave, with Kyle bringing up the rear.

As they took the first turn in Jasmine's directions, they encountered a group of seven Protheon workers headed for the same stairwell.

"Stars! What happened to him?" one of the women exclaimed when she saw Dave being carried.

"The alarm must have spooked him," Kira replied. "I think he tripped and hit his head. We found him on the floor like this."

The woman's face dropped. "The elevators are locked down. Can you get him down the stairs?"

"I've got him, don't worry," Ari said. The soldier took Dave's full weight, slinging his legs over one arm and cradling his shoulders with the other.

"I'm sure a medic will respond to the alarm," Kira said to the group of Protheon workers.

"Go on ahead," a man in the group said, gesturing Kira's team toward the stairwell.

"Thanks." Kira ran ahead to prop the door open while Ari carried Dave through.

She exchanged glances with Nia while she passed by with Kyle.

<I know how she feels,> Jasmine said. *<Someone could realize we don't work here at any moment.>*

<Our forged credentials have gotten us this far. Besides, we don't have any other options. A roof extraction was a no-go, and it's not like there's a backdoor we could take. Going out the front is our only play.>

<But having more people see us?>

<*Sometimes it's easier to hide in plain sight,*> Kira replied.

They descended the staircase from their current position on the sixth floor. The Protheon facility was like any of the private industry structures Kira had ventured into over her career with the Guard, with sophisticated common areas and emergency stairwells cast in plain concrete with steel stairs. She could have been anywhere, for all the distinguishing features of the stairwell. In some ways, that was a poetic expression of her covert ops activities—same mission, different bad guys, different place.

Despite Ari carrying Dave, the group made fast time on the descent. The Protheon employees were only a few steps behind, so Kira elected to remain silent.

When they reached the bottom of the stairwell, Nia opened the doorway and ushered Ari through, followed by Kira and Kyle.

Kira scanned the lobby, looking for the right place to deposit Dave.

Employees were pouring out of other stairwells into the lobby, and the bank of elevators had a red 'X' above each door. Half a dozen employees dressed in orange vests were shouting instructions for people to head outside.

That's as good a target as any. Kira bobbed her head toward one of the orange-vested women nearest their stairwell, and she broke into a light jog, headed in that direction.

Ari followed her lead.

"He just collapsed!" Kira exclaimed as she approached the target woman with Ari.

The soldier set Dave on the floor.

"Did you see what happened?" the woman asked, concern clouding her face and she looked over Dave's unconscious form.

"No, but we thought we should get him out of there when we heard the alarm," Kira said. "I'll see if I can find a medic. Check over there," she said to Ari, nodding toward the corner of the lobby opposite their current position.

"Stay with him," Ari told the woman.

The Protheon worker knelt over Dave while Kira and Ari disappeared into the crowd.

Kira lost sight of her team in an attempt to blend in with the flow of traffic heading outside.

<Shite, we weren't supposed to get separated,> she said to Jasmine.

<Everyone knows the rendezvous. Just get us there.>

The throng of people flooding from the fourteen-story building directed Kira out through the lobby doors into a well-landscaped pavilion. A fountain filled the center of a circular drive, which led to the main roadway a kilometer to the east.

She blinked in the sudden midday sun—a harsher light there on Dakar than she was used to in her home system.

People gravitated toward a grassy field to the left of the entry driveway, presumably a predetermined evacuation site.

Kira, however, headed toward the left as inconspicuously as she could, toward a pathway that led through an opening between two low hills to the employee parking lot. There was no cover available between Protheon's entry and the path, but she walked with purpose.

Ten meters ahead, she spotted Kyle and Nia hustling in the same direction.

"You can't head home. We need to do a roll call!" a man shouted behind Kira.

<Is he talking to us?>

<Pretend you don't hear him,> Jasmine suggested.

Kira picked up her pace.

"Hey!"

<Stars, he's persistent!> Kira hazarded a glance behind her.

The man was jogging in her direction. "Meeting area is back this way," he called.

Kyle and Nia were almost to the pass between the hills. Once inside, they'd be able to disappear.

Kira spotted Ari twelve meters to her right, following the edge of the circular drive. She didn't notice anyone watching him at the moment, so the best bet was to allow him to make a clean escape.

She stopped. "I already checked in with my floor marshal," she stated without turning around.

"We need a headcount," he insisted.

Except I'd be an extra. Kira took a slow breath, noting that Ari was about to pass into the pathway between the hills. "My dog is in my car. I need to walk her," she said.

"Wha…?"

<Jasmine, how do you feel about trying out my new super-speed?>

<We haven't practiced enough. This isn't an advisable time to experiment.>

<It's the perfect time.>

Kira bolted for the pathway. Her perception shifted so every footstep seemed like it was in slow motion relative to her surroundings. She looked back over her shoulder and saw the man raising his hands in frustrated protest, but the movement was barely perceptible.

She returned her focus ahead and ran. Though the world around her didn't seem to move, each of her steps was at a normal running pace from her vantage. In what seemed like six seconds, she caught up to Ari, just as he was rounding the bend in the pathway between the hills where he would be hidden from the pursuer.

Kira returned to normal speed. Her heart pounded in her ears—not from exertion, but from exhilaration.

Ari did a double-take when she appeared next to him. "How did you get here so fast?"

"Putting my new abilities to use. Come on, we need to hurry." She continued running alongside him at a brisk pace.

Kyle and Nia were waiting at the entrance to the employee parking lot.

"We'll be all over the security footage," Kyle muttered as soon as Kira was within earshot.

"And they won't be able to connect us to anything, aside from the mock profiles behind our forged credentials. That's precisely why we had visitor badges," she replied.

"I'm going to vote against future ops where we have to dress like this," Nia said with a downward glance of distaste at her attire.

"Agreed." Ari flexed in his business suit. "We're supposed to be covert ops, not playing dress-up and impersonating people."

Kira sighed. "It's not like this was the first time we've done this."

"Yeah, well, I guess I got used to being shot at," Nia replied. "And getting to shoot back."

"That's definitely more fun," Ari agreed.

"That's precisely what's going to happen if you keep standing here and complaining. Move!" Kira shooed them toward the back of the parking lot, where their stealthed shuttle was waiting for them.

As they approached the shuttle, Kyle made entries on his wrist controls to open the back hatch. They piled inside. Kyle and Nia went to the cockpit while Kira and Ari strapped into the back.

"So, things didn't go quite as we planned, but we got what we came for," Kira commented.

"Glad it's *your* job to explain that to Sandren," Nia said while she powered up the shuttle.

"It won't be an issue," Kira assured her team. *At least, I hope not.*

<It could have gone better,> Jasmine interjected. *<You took some unnecessary risks.>*

<Maybe they're right—I've gotten used to the firefights, too.>

<We need to work on your appetite for drama.>

The problem was, Kira wasn't sure she wanted it to go away. She decided to keep that notion to herself.

The shuttle lifted off from the ground and launched into space.

Stealthed in orbit, the *Raven* was awaiting their return. The shuttle slipped into its berth in the belly of the larger ship.

"Good work, team," Kira said while disembarking the shuttle. "I'll see you after my debrief with Major Sandren."

"I'm telling you, he's going to be pissed," Nia said with a slow shake of her head.

Kira shrugged. "Maybe, but I doubt it."

"Here's the drive." Kyle handed their bounty to her. "Hope it goes well."

"Thanks. See you in a few."

Kira jogged toward the ladder that led up from the bay to the deck housing the galley, living quarters, and Sandren's office.

"What the fok was that alarm about?" Sandren demanded as soon as Kira's head cleared the floor of the ladder shaft.

She gulped. *Okay, so maybe this won't be as easy a conversation as I thought.*

CHAPTER 2

"HELLO, SIR." KIRA finished scaling the ladder and then clasped her hands behind her back.

"My office. Now." Major Sandren stormed down the corridor.

<I know we deviated a little, but isn't he overreacting?> Kira asked Jasmine.

<I'm sure you'll know his exact thinking any moment.>

Kira wasn't particularly eager to find out. She followed the major into his office and closed the door.

Sandren stood behind his desk, resting his hands on the back of his chair while leaning forward. "Please explain to me how and why you evacuated the entire facility that you were supposed to be in and out of without causing any disturbance?"

Kira took a slow breath and met his gaze. "Well, sir, we had to abandon the original plan as soon as we got inside. Our badges got us through the front door just fine, but when we reached the communications room, it was occupied."

"Dealing with one individual should be well within your

skillset."

"Yes, sir." She nodded. "He was belligerent, but we easily subdued him. I glanced at his mind and quickly determined he didn't know anything pertinent to our mission, so we bound and gagged him. Nia and Kyle proceeded to retrieve the information."

"What about the alarm?" Sandren prompted.

"We got some unexpected additional company, so I improvised."

The major wiped his hand down his face. "Captain, going from one bound individual to triggering an evacuation alarm for a whole building isn't just improvising—it's changing the whole foking plan!"

"The more people who came to question us, the quicker our cover would have fallen apart. The fastest way to get out was to blend in with the many other people who were leaving."

"Except you were seen parting ways from the group of evacuees. Plus, we had very intentional reasons for sending you in the way we did. This disturbance upset plans beyond this one operation."

Kira looked down. "You didn't inform me about those other activities, sir."

He glared at her. "I shouldn't *have* to. If you had followed orders, it wouldn't have been relevant."

"With all due respect, sir, plans need to change on the fly more often than not. If there were critical activities tangential to this op, then telling me would have allowed me to make a more informed decision."

Sandren sighed. "Kira, I know this has been a difficult month and a half for you, but your new abilities don't entitle you to break the rules. We have a chain of command and mission orders for a reason. Consider this your official warning."

<Is he serious? Threatening to bench me because we pulled the fire alarm?>

<Kira, don't talk back. Nod and smile,> Jasmine cautioned.

<This is absurd, right? He—>

<Now is not the time or place. You're still on an endorphin high. You can have a conversation with him when you've mellowed out.>

Kira took a deep breath. "Yes, sir. Understood."

"I expect your full written report in four hours. Dismissed." Sandren sat down in his chair with a huff.

<Why don't we keep the details of this meeting between us for now,> Kira suggested to Jasmine.

<Works for me.>

She exited the major's office and then headed for the washroom. The only thing worse than getting reprimanded by her superior officer was having it happen while she was out of uniform. Getting back into her shipsuit was top priority.

Just as she touched the washroom door's handle, the hallway lights flickered.

"The fok…?" Kira froze.

<Power fluctuation,> Jasmine reported. *<No apparent cause in the ship's real-time performance report.>*

<Maybe it was a glitch.>

The lights flickered again. *<This isn't normal.>*

<Kira, I recommend you get into your shipsuit immediately, in case we lose life support.>

<I was just thinking the same thing.> Kira quickly opened the door and raced into the washroom.

The three members of her team were drying off in the showers.

"Don't suppose you saw the lights flicker?" Kyle asked.

"It was doing it in the hall, too," Kira confirmed. "Power fluctuations ship-wide."

"I told you it wasn't the steam messing with the overhead fixture!" Nia ran toward her locker.

"Get dressed," Kira encouraged her team. "It might be nothing, but if we have an issue, we need to be prepared."

"Foking great." Ari ran for his own locker.

Kyle followed suit.

"How'd it go with Sandren?" Nia asked while she dressed.

"Fine," Kira replied, grabbing her shipsuit. "We'll get in our mission reports and explain what happened."

Nia eyed her. "He was pissed, wasn't he?"

Kira kept her gaze focused inside her locker. "We accomplished our mission."

"Yep, thought so." Nia finished securing her shipsuit and closed her locker door. "I'm going to take a nap. Wake me up if the ship is rapidly decompressing."

"I'll join you," Ari said, following her from the washroom.

Kyle hung back and waited for the door to close behind their two comrades.

"Are you okay, Kira?"

She finished securing her shipsuit and then slumped against her locker. "I messed up again. That's two major fok-ups in two months—all since this foking Robus thing."

"You're being too hard on yourself," her friend responded. "Not to sound like a dick, but you were far from perfect before."

"Yeah, thanks." She scoffed and shook her head.

"I mean that you're hyper-aware of everything now," he continued. "All of us have made plenty of mistakes and wrong calls on ops over the years, but now you're scrutinizing every action because you've undergone this change. Are you honestly saying that Sandren never gave you any reprimands before this transformation?"

Kira thought for a moment. "I guess he did."

<You had four 'harshly worded' performance reviews prior to my pairing with you,> Jasmine stated.

<And you still elected to join me?>

<You were too fascinating a case for me to pass up,> the AI replied. *<Plus, I knew I'd be getting involved with someone a little out there when you agreed to our pairing without any proper time to get to know each other.>*

<Sandren and Kaen recommended you; that was enough.>

Jasmine was silent for a moment. *<If Major Sandren's opinion carries so much weight that you'd allow him to select an AI for you, no wonder you take his criticism of your performance to heart.>*

<Yeah, I guess I do,> Kira realized.

She returned her attention to Kyle. "You're right. I've always been worried about letting my team down, but I worry about it more now. While I'm figuring out this new self, I have to hold myself to a higher standard."

"There's being cautious, and then there's crippling yourself with self-doubt," Kyle replied. "After you showed the Trols who was boss, you seemed so confident."

"And then I remembered that cockiness gets people killed, so I adjusted my attitude." Kira crossed her arms. "But maybe I swung too far in the other direction."

"No one is perfect, Kira." Kyle stepped over to her and placed a reassuring hand on her shoulder. "Robus or not, you're still a person. No one expects you to always be right."

"But I'm expected to not pull alarms in buildings where we're not supposed to be, apparently," Kira muttered.

"Hey, it got us out of there. I thought it was—"

The lights cut out.

"Shite!" Kira groped in the dark for the emergency kit next to the lockers.

"Why aren't they coming back on?" Kyle asked. His question was followed by a bang on the locker doors as his hand found them for spatial reference.

"Your guess is as good as mine."

Kira's fingers finally located the latch to the emergency kit, and she opened it. Inside, she felt around for the cool, metal cylinder of a flashlight.

"Watch your eyes," she warned, then clicked on the device. Red light flooded the washroom.

"We still have gravity," Kyle observed. "What might—"

The main lights flickered on again.

Kira blinked rapidly as her eyes adjusted. "This whole being-in-the-middle-of-nowhere-on-a-malfunctioning-spaceship thing isn't working for me."

"That makes two of us."

"Attention," Rodrick, the *Raven*'s captain, announced over the central comm system. "You've no doubt noticed the power fluctuations over the past five minutes. We have reset the central command modules, and all systems appear to be functioning properly. We will alert you if we detect any further anomalous activity. In the meantime, please proceed as normal. Thank you."

Kira and Kyle looked at each other.

"Uh, that makes it even weirder, yeah?" she said.

He nodded. "What aren't they telling us?"

She shook her head. "I have no idea, but I can't wait to be back home."

— — —

After the second flicker of the overhead lights and the touch-surface desk, Colonel Terence Kaen was certain something at Orion Station was amiss.

He rose from his desk and jogged to the office door, peeking out into the hallway. Sure enough, the flickering extended everywhere he could see from his vantage. *What's going on?*

Kaen returned to his desk and activated the comm. "Major, are you seeing this?" he asked.

"If you mean the power fluctuations that aren't showing up in any of the system performance dashboard, then yes," Major Deanna Olvera, the security chief, replied.

"Is it internal or an external attack?" Kaen questioned.

"I'd tell you if I knew. We're trying to figure it out." Olvera paused. "Excuse me, sir, General Lucian is calling."

"I'll be standing by if you need me," Kaen said.

"Yes, sir."

The comm link ended.

If General Lucian is calling the chief of security, then something is definitely going on. Kaen frowned.

He hated having to sit back and wait for instructions, but he could offer no assistance or insights to the technical specialists. All the same, he felt like he needed to do *something*.

Unexpected anxiety gripped his chest. He hadn't experienced that feeling since—

No, it's not possible... He froze in the middle of his office, on his way back to his desk. The disquiet tickling the back of his mind was the same unease he'd felt when Nox had jumped into Jared—when the Trols were close and attempting to exert their control.

He dismissed it. *No, they're gone. And they controlled people, not computers.*

Such flashes of panic hit him occasionally, when something seemed amiss. He would think he had come to terms with his experience of being possessed by an alien captor, but then he'd have a random reaction like this and be reminded that he wasn't over it at all.

Traces of the trauma lingered, and would continue to linger. He'd been through an ordeal that had changed him.

Separate the anxiety from the facts, he told himself.

In this case, the facts were that Orion Station was experiencing a computer glitch. There was nothing to point to the Trols, or any other foe. More likely, it was a bad connection at one of the power relay nodes—or whatever it had been when the same thing happened a year prior. Machines were fallible, but they'd fix this issue just like they'd fixed every other malfunction.

With his mind set at ease, Kaen settled back behind his desk. The lights hadn't shuddered for two minutes. If there was cause for future concern, they'd let him know.

— — —

Home at last. Kira breathed a sigh of relief.

Returning from a mission had always been rewarding, but it was even more special now that Leon was a permanent resident at Orion Station. Though they'd only been together for two months on this second go-around, their history together as teenagers had allowed them to quickly fall into the routine of an established couple.

In that tradition, Kira was pleased to find him waiting for her outside the door to her quarters.

"Hey, you," he greeted with a warm smile that lit up his violet eyes.

Her heart melted in spite of herself. "Hey."

She had learned many years before that a sense of 'home' was more about the company she kept than any particular physical location. And Leon had become part of that home. Being with both him and her Guard family completed her world.

Leon drew her in for a kiss as soon as she was within arm's reach. "I missed you."

"Missed you, too." Kira palmed open her door using the biometric lock. She ushered Leon inside.

"How did the op go?" he asked, following her direction.

"We got what we needed, but we made a bit of a scene."

He chuckled. "That's becoming a trademark of yours."

"Yeah, it is." She closed the door and dropped her travel bag on the ground. "Problem is, we're supposed to be *covert* ops."

"No offense, but your new abilities don't exactly help you blend in."

"Honestly, I think that's part of my problem."

Kira collapsed on her bed, and Leon sat down next to her.

"Did you want to talk about it?" he asked.

"Not right now, but thanks." She smiled weakly. "I had hoped things would get back to normal as soon as I had Jasmine to help regulate my transformations, but the new 'normal' isn't quite what I'd thought it'd be."

Leon tilted his head. "What were you expecting?"

"I dunno." She looked down. "I didn't think I'd have to keep proving myself."

His brow knitted. "You don't have to prove yourself to anyone."

"I do. Constantly. I had wanted to show that I'm not a liability after these changes, but instead, I keep finding evidence that maybe I *am*."

"Try to talk some sense into her, Leon," Jasmine chimed in over the audible comms. "I've been attempting to get her to hear reason for the past six hours, but she won't snap out of this funk."

"I've been careless and impulsive since I got these nanites," Kira insisted. "That's reason to be concerned—especially since you're supposed to be the one keeping an eye on me, but you keep saying everything is okay."

"Isn't the fact that I'm telling you you're fine the reassurance you need? I *do* question you when I feel it's prudent," Jasmine replied.

Concern flitted across Leon's face. "I'm not sure if I should get involved in this or not…"

"Jasmine is butting in on personal time when she shouldn't." Kira glared at the AI in her mind.

<Fine, I'll leave you be,> Jasmine said privately. *<But we need to get to the bottom of these feelings, Kira. You'll never be able to maximize the use of your new abilities if you keep having these doubts.>*

<Yeah, I know,> Kira acknowledged. "Sorry, I don't mean for you to get caught in the middle of things with me and Jasmine," she said to Leon.

"Sometimes I feel like I have two girlfriends now." He laughed.

Kira snorted. "Oh, stars! Right! Don't say that to Jasmine when she's not under explicit instructions to stay quiet."

Leon eyed her. "Do I detect a hint of jealousy?"

"That would require me to have a concern about her taking you away from me. Since we share this body, she wouldn't get very far."

"I also know better than to date other scientist-types,"

Leon said. "Get two biologists together, and you can *really* overanalyze a relationship in the wrong ways."

"Speaking from experience?"

"Second-hand. I watched it play out several times while I was in grad school. Wasn't pretty."

Kira winced. "Yikes."

"I'll take this complementary thing we have going on. It works." He took her hand.

"Well, good, because I don't particularly want to share you."

"Stars, you *are* jealous!" Leon laughed.

She blushed. "I can't help it! You got me started down the mental path of someone trying to take you away from me, and—"

Leon looked her in the eyes. "Kira, I love you, but you're being crazy right now. And I mean that in the nicest way possible."

"I am, aren't I?" She sighed.

He stroked the side of her face. "You seem off. Did something happen?"

"Nothing that should have me acting like this." She thought about it. "I dunno, there's just this... feeling."

"That doesn't give me a lot to go on."

She groaned. "I know. Just..." She stood up from the bed and paced in front of him. "This is going to sound even more nuts, but I've been fighting this feeling of impending doom."

"Kira..."

"I know! I know. But you asked, so there it is. I keep fearing I'm going to do something that's going to get people hurt. So whenever there's a little glitch, or whatever, my first thought is, 'This is the thing that's going to bring my new world crashing down.' "

Leon stood up and wrapped his arms around her. "You're driving yourself crazy over nothing."

"*Is* it nothing? I sounded an alarm today as an exit strategy for a covert op."

"That actually sounds like a great way to get out of a building."

She frowned. "Yeah, see, that's what I thought. Sandren disagrees."

"If that's the only thing that's bothering you, then you are *really* making a bigger deal out of it than you should." Leon caught her gaze. "We all do things that, in retrospect, we would have done differently. Learn from the experience and move on."

"I know. That's what Jasmine has been saying."

"So listen to us." He smiled. "What's the point of surrounding yourself with smart people if you ignore everything they have to say?"

"Okay, okay." She returned his smile. "Sorry I was acting weird. I think it's just one of those days where a bunch of little things have added up, you know?"

"I've been there. Don't worry about it." He gave her a light kiss.

She kissed him back, then pulled away to retrieve her travel bag from the floor. "I need to take a quick shower. I didn't get one on the *Raven* because of this weird power fluctuation. Didn't want to be without my suit in the event it turned into a bigger issue."

Leon's face dropped. "When was that?"

"Right when we were leaving Dakar. Six hours ago, maybe. Why?"

"We had some flickering light action here at the base right around then," Leon revealed.

"This is *not* helping the paranoia I'm trying to keep at bay."

Leon placed his hands on her upper arms. "They didn't make an announcement, there was no alarm, and we're still alive. It's probably nothing. Forget I said anything."

Kira nodded. "Right, coincidence." She forced a smile. "I'll get cleaned up, and then maybe we can grab dinner later?"

"Sounds great. I have a couple things to finish up at the lab, but then I'm free for the rest of the night."

"Okay, I'll message you in a bit." Kira kissed him. "Thanks again for talking some sense into me. You're much better at it than Jasmine."

"I've also known you a lot longer."

"You do know me well. Maybe *too* well." She narrowed her eyes playfully.

Leon smiled back. "Ah, the gift of history—being able to use your own arguments against you."

"Watch it, mister. That goes both ways!"

"A fact I know all too well. See you soon." With a parting hug, Leon went to attend to his remaining tasks.

<*Sorry,*> Kira said to Jasmine when they were alone. <*Sometimes I need to hear things from a source outside my own head.*>

<*That history does mean a lot. We'll get there. I can't compete with someone you've known for more than a decade.*>

<*Thanks, Jasmine. I do value your opinion. I'm just stubborn.*>

The AI laughed in her mind. <*That's putting it mildly.*>

Kira paused. <*Not to feed back into my worries, but do you know any more about that power fluctuation here?*>

<*I looked up the records as soon as he mentioned it. It was dismissed as a faulty converter.*>

<*But it's odd, right? The timing with the* Raven?>

<I agree that it is,> Jasmine replied. <I can't venture a guess at what a connection between the two events might mean.>

<So, pretend like it's nothing?>

<Right now, it is nothing,> the AI pointed out. <We have noted curious data points, but until there is enough information to perform a proper analysis, we cannot draw any correlation, causation, or trends.>

Kira chuckled. <Leon may be better at appealing to my emotions, but you can win any battle of logic.>

<Thank you, Kira. That's a touching compliment.>

<One of these days, I'll learn I should never try to argue.> Deep down, she knew her stubbornness was too engrained. A lively discussion was part of the fun.

CHAPTER 3

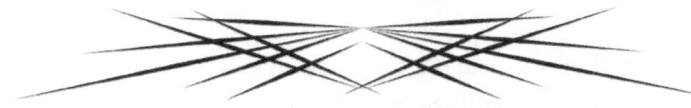

I WISH KIRA weren't so hard on herself, Leon thought while he made his way back to the research lab. *I've been here for less than two months. My external validation shouldn't be necessary.*

There was more to it than just the time together in recent weeks, though. The history that afforded them immediate comfort with one another also brought with it the potential to fall into old habits.

He was sure she didn't realize it, but Leon suspected that her recent transformation—and her reconnection with him— had triggered Kira to reflect on her past, perhaps all the way back to her original decision to join the Guard. The validation she was seeking for her recent command decisions was likely rooted in a deeper desire to validate her career path; she wasn't questioning a single decision, but rather every decision leading up to that recent moment. He'd been catching hints of it over the past six weeks, and seeing her ongoing evaluation of her own command decisions reinforced his hypothesis.

In his short time observing Kira in the Guard, he had no doubt that she was in her element. There was no reason for her to question her decision to join the Guard, because it was where she belonged. Somehow, he needed to help her recapture her self-assurance.

Tackling that challenge would take time, however. Confidence needed to be rebuilt from within. All he could do for now was be supportive in her moments of doubt, in the way he knew she would be for him. Mutual trust, respect, love— their foundation would see them through any future trials they may face.

Though it was nearing the end of the day, Leon found that Tess and Jack were still absorbed in their work when he arrived at the lab.

"Welcome back," Tess greeted. The stickers around her monitor had continued to multiply over the past month, to the point that a rainbow space pony had become a permanent fixture on any document she happened to have open on the screen.

"Sorry to have ditched you in the middle of the analysis," Leon replied.

"I know better than to ignore a girlfriend's call. You're good," Jack said with a slight smile, glancing up from the monitor at his own immaculate workstation.

"Latest model finished running a couple minutes ago," Tess reported.

Leon came to attention. "Did you review it yet?"

"Nope, waiting for you."

"All right, let's take a look."

Leon had been analyzing material samples from the Gaelon System for the past month, scouring fragments from the dwarf planet for any genetic or biological remnants. They'd also looked at samples from the gas giant to gain a better understanding of how the bioamplifier functioned.

All of their research had made it painfully clear how little they knew. With each dead-end analysis, new questions had led down increasingly convoluted lines of reasoning. Whenever Leon was ready to admit how much they didn't know and leave things be, they'd make a discovery that would encourage them to keep pressing forward.

Right now, he needed one of those wins.

"Well, shite." Leon whistled through his teeth.

Tess shook her head with wonder. "When did finding nothing become so exciting?"

The most recent round of assessment had been a shot in the dark: running a comprehensive comparison of the materials they'd already catalogued in Gaelon against the list of minerals and biological samples from worlds in the Empire's database, including the Priesthood's formerly sealed archives. Getting *access* to that database alone had required Kaen pulling some strings, but the permission had been granted earlier that week.

In the time since, they'd been running batches of data, trying to locate the sources of the materials found in the artificial world, since the minerals mined from Mysar and Valta could only account for a fraction of the dwarf planet's composition. They figured that tracing back those materials to other sources may offer some insight into where the Trols had originally come from or what kind of places others of their kind might target in the future, if there were more.

What the analysis revealed, however, was that none of the samples could be traced to any known world.

"They're from outside Empire space," Leon murmured.

"Or maybe even outside this *galaxy*," Tess emphasized.

"How do they travel?" Leon mused aloud. "We have yet to see any evidence of a propulsion system."

"Maybe they have a different way of initiating a subspace jump," Jack chimed in from across the lab. "I mean, they communicate telepathically through some kind of subspace connection."

"There's still the issue of how they move through normal space once in-system. If they don't use a conventional propulsion system, then that leaves... what, teleporting?" Leon shook his head. "That's crazy, right?"

Jack raised an eyebrow. "More crazy than body-snatching telepathic nano-aliens that live in kilometer-deep pits?"

Leon sighed. "I keep revising my definition of 'out there' and then promptly forget that reality and insanity are now one in the same."

"It's our burden." Tess smiled. "I would like to note, however, that we got an almost-hit on one of the organisms in the mix on that gas giant."

"Really? That's new." Leon tilted his head.

"I don't think it's an origin match but rather an indicator of type. The microorganisms from Gaelon were definitely genetically engineered, but I think they were modeled after the sort that have thrived on Rylon II and Salwell IV," she continued. "As far as we know, the life of those gas giants came about through natural means—which suggests that there could be other systems in the outskirts of the galaxy where similar life has emerged."

"That doesn't help explain how the Trols learned to manipulate those genetic codes to modify the microorganisms for their own needs," Leon said.

"But it does support our working hypothesis that the Trols only adapt technology and biology they come across, rather than generating anything truly original of their own," Tess replied.

Which doesn't bode well for them having gotten their hands on our external processor. Leon wouldn't dare say that aloud to anyone, especially Kira. It was that field mistake that had precipitated her lack of faith in her command decisions. Even her successful takedown of the dwarf planet in Gaelon using only her telepathic powers hadn't been enough to reaffirm her abilities as a Guard officer in her mind.

Everyone had hoped that the external processor had been destroyed in Gaelon along with the planet, closing the issue. But, if Jack's hunch was correct and the Trols maintained a subspace link that extended beyond remote mind control, then they could have communicated the details of the computer operations at the core of the Empire's technology. Any groups of Trols that existed elsewhere might now have that information.

Leon suppressed the thought, knowing that following the hypothetical would only generate as yet unfounded fears about his civilization being conquered by new, invisible alien overlords.

"Well," he pushed back from his computer terminal, "I guess we can definitively say now that we know the Trols come from somewhere remote and unexplored."

"New life, unlike anything discovered elsewhere." Tess was almost radiant from the revelation.

Leon had learned over the past month that she specialized in xenobiology, which in retrospect seemed obvious, given the comments she'd made in their previous collaborations. It was also no wonder she'd accepted him as a team leader, given he came from Valta—regarded as one of the most biologically diverse and unique worlds within the grasp of the Taran Empire.

"Exciting stuff," Leon agreed. "I wish we had answers to offer, but at least now we know to look outward to learn more, rather than inward."

"Yes, there is that." Tess was silent for a moment. "Do you think they'll come back?"

Jack snorted. "Would you come back if someone blew up *your* planet-sized base?"

That could have been the equivalent of a tiny outpost, for all we know. Leon decided to keep that thought to himself, too.

"If they come back, at least we know more about them now. Between the sound frequency and the chemical mixture to dissolve valteron, that's a decent defensive strategy."

"I hope so." Tess' tone lacked its normal enthusiasm.

"Did you find something else?" Leon asked her, wondering where the change in mood was stemming from.

"Just thinking back to that weirdness with the lights earlier. Last time something went wonky in the station, Kaen was possessed by Nox."

"We've checked him, he's clean," Leon assured her. "And we've checked everyone else."

Tess opened her mouth like she was about to make a counterpoint, but she nodded instead.

"Let's not worry about that right now," he continued. "I have a couple of things to finish up, but then let's call it an early night."

"Works for me," Jack replied.

Tess smiled. "You owe me a drink! I told you the Trols were from outside Empire territory."

"Yes, you did," Leon conceded. "A bet's a bet."

— — —

After a month on Mysar, Ellen had acclimated to the warmer environment. She still hated it—and would complain about the heat every chance she got—but at least it no longer wiped her out the second she left a dome.

Her temporary office space inside the Mysaran government building in the city was beginning to feel more like her own than the desk waiting for her back on Elusia. Based on the quizzical look President Joris gave her each time they checked in, she was sure he suspected as much, too.

The twice-weekly video calls provided a chance for her to update him on her progress in rebuilding the Mysaran government, after it was gutted following the revelation that the Trol alien Reya had been in control of the Mysaran chancellor. Ellen had thought it would take a week, maybe two, to identify appropriate individuals to fill the power vacuum left by the removal of the planet's leaders; in her prior experience, someone was always eager for a chance to advance.

This time, though, no one was rising to the occasion.

The only people who'd demonstrated genuine interest in her efforts were Trisha, Fiona, and Edgar, but the latter two had made it *very* clear they had no interest in being chancellor. While Trisha hadn't outright rejected the idea, she didn't have the résumé to support an appointment on that level.

After a month of interviews and searching for other candidates, Ellen was beginning to wonder if she'd need to look offworld to find someone.

As she met President Joris' gaze over the video call for their latest check-in, she pondered whether it was finally time to share that concern.

"Was there something else?" Joris prompted. He raised a fair eyebrow above his blue eyes.

"Well," Ellen began, "we've spent most of our time talking

about infrastructure and getting trade between Elusia and Mysar back on track. While those operations have resumed, and seem to be going well, there's still the issue of restoring the government leadership."

"I thought you were conducting interviews with potential candidates?"

"Yeah…" she hedged. "I mean, I have been, yes. But I'm pretty much out of people to talk to."

Joris folded his hands on his desktop. "Are you being too picky?"

She laughed. "Oh, I wish that was the case! No, sir, I set bare minimum qualifications to get an initial list going—there are some baseline credentials we can't compromise. But everyone I've talked to who meets those basic requirements isn't interested."

"I find that difficult to believe. Every time I run for re-election, there's always some new contender, however unqualified, eager to unseat me."

"That's just it, sir—I can't find someone *qualified* who wants it. A handful of disgruntled miners have come forward with vocal opposition to the current system, demanding we launch a military assault on Elusia or relocate to Valta."

The presidents' eyes widened. "Really? I haven't seen anything about that."

Ellen cracked a smile. "Well, I *am* the press secretary, remember? I know how to contain an unfavorable story."

"I agree that we couldn't have someone with that level of bias in command, but I'm concerned that there's still a vocal separatist movement on Mysar. I thought that most people on the world had begun advocating for unity in the Elvar Trinary as soon as Hale's influence was removed."

She nodded. "Publicly, yes. But there are going to be those

that disagree, no matter what topic, or where it is. It's the voice of hundreds versus tens of thousands."

Joris leaned back in his chair. "What do you propose?"

"I…" Ellen faded out. *This is as good of an opening as I'll get.*

She took a deep breath. "I believe we need to think bigger than Mysar, sir. If no one on this world wants to step up as a leader, then perhaps it's time we consider a unified government for the Elvar Trinary."

"Hmm."

I expected more of a reaction than that… Ellen eyed him. "Sir?"

"I've been wondering when you'd make that suggestion."

She smiled. "Was it that obvious that's where things were headed?"

"Inevitable progress," he replied. "I've given it some thought. The Elvar Trinary would have greater negotiating power and presence with the Empire if we were three united worlds rather than just Elusia as a single planet. One political face of the system, with leaders on each planet for domestic issues—perhaps with a 'governor' title."

" 'Governor' might be an easier sell to potential candidates than 'chancellor'," Ellen acknowledged.

"Moreover, the restructure would simplify the trade agreements. You mentioned that the lingering hang-ups are all related to tariffs."

She nodded. "And with a unified government, there'd be no reason to try to make money off of each other."

"Precisely."

"Hmm." *Okay, so maybe there's more depth to that reaction than I thought.*

"See if you can subtly present the idea and gauge the

response. If it's favorable, we can discuss a more formal political strategy to gain public buy-in."

"Yes, sir."

"I'll speak to you next week." Joris ended the call.

Ellen slumped back in her office chair, pivoting around to gaze out the window.

I think he already has someone in mind for the Mysaran governor, she mused while watching the people go about their lives on the streets below. *And I think it may be me.*

She wasn't sure how she felt about that idea. While her qualifications did exceed the minimums she'd established for her interview purposes, she hardly considered herself a qualified candidate. She wasn't born on Mysar, and she didn't embody the culture of the world.

Plus, she'd already sworn her allegiance to Elusia.

Joris knows that. He wouldn't consider me for governor. Her initial thought seemed ridiculous the more she thought about it.

However, the change in title offered new flexibility in the job qualifications. Ellen ran through the candidates she'd previously dismissed. The governor should be a native of Mysar—someone with a vested interest in the world. She had yet to come across anyone who cared as much as Trisha Mercer.

Stars! Though Trisha wasn't quite ready for chancellor, she would be great as a governor, if I could convince her.

She had the makings of a leader who could be embraced by the people—born to an average middle-class family, volunteered with charities, and had earned her present position in the government through hard work and dedication. Moreover, she had a good heart. While she could use some toughening, the right foundation was there.

All Ellen had to do was persuade her to take the job.

— — —

Repairing trust after an op that didn't go well was a tricky endeavor, but it was a critical component of making sure her team was ready for anything. Having had time to reflect on the Protheon mission and the decisions she'd made in the field, Kira was confident she'd made the right calls, given the information at her disposal.

The matter was worth a follow-up discussion with Major Sandren, though she'd have to be careful to keep the conversation from devolving into an 'I told you so' exchange. Her unique abilities didn't change her position in the chain of command.

As soon as she had showered, Kira decided that she should talk with the major before her dinner with Leon. The longer she delayed the conversation, the more awkward it would be.

She checked one of the monitors along the hall walls and saw that Sandren was in his office, right where Kira had hoped he'd be.

She traversed the station along the familiar path, organizing her thoughts.

When she arrived, the door was open, and Sandren was working at his desk.

He glanced up. "Captain, what brings you by?"

"Sir, I wanted to discuss the last op. We didn't end our previous exchange on the best of terms."

He nodded. "Come in and have a seat."

Kira stepped into the office and closed the door behind her. "I apologize for dropping in unannounced."

"Not at all. I'm glad you came by."

She looked down at her hands, then brought her gaze up

to meet Sandren's. "Sir, I wanted to apologize for my behavior earlier. I acted rashly without regard for the consequences."

The major softened. "After going through the mission recording Jasmine provided from her observations, I've reevaluated my stance. With more people converging on your location, it was unlikely you would have been able to retreat without needing to shoot others."

Kira's heart leaped. "Sir?"

"You have good instincts, Captain. I shouldn't have doubted you."

<*See? Told you,*> Jasmine said in Kira's mind.

"Thank you, sir. Having your trust means a great deal to me. I hated to think that I'd let you down."

"I've always been hard on you, Kira, but that's because I know you can take it. Even before the changes from these nanites, you were capable of more than you gave yourself credit for. What you lacked in physical prowess, you more than made up for in spirit. You would never have had this command if it wasn't for your quick thinking. I shouldn't have passed judgment without understanding the scenario."

"All the same, this was an important reminder that our actions aren't isolated," she replied. "I acted in the interest of my team in that moment without concern for the ripple effects."

"It did complicate other matters, I won't lie," Sandren admitted. "However, the information you retrieved will allow us to set it right. No long-term harm done."

"I'm relieved to hear it, sir."

"I've said before that you should trust your instincts. It would do me good to remember my own words."

She smiled. "Yes, sir."

He smiled back. "Thank you for stopping by. I've always

appreciated your strength of character to approach conflict head-on."

"Gladly, sir. I'll be standing by for our next assignment."

"It might be a few days. We're having the *Raven* checked out. Apparently, the issues we experienced weren't isolated."

Kira frowned. "Leon mentioned that there was an incident here at base."

"Reports from other ships, too," Sandren revealed. "The technical team is looking into it. Nothing we can do for now but wait for their report."

"Yes, sir."

"Have a good night, Kira."

Kira bid him farewell. As she opened the door, the lights cut out for a second, then re-illuminated brighter than their typical output.

Sandren's desktop screen flickered between its normal data display and bits of gibberish code.

Kira's gaze met Sandren's. "Shite, what now?"

CHAPTER 4

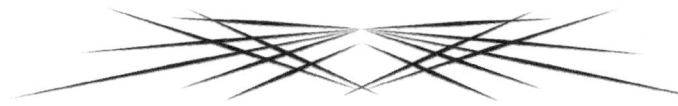

KAEN EXITED THE administrative wing of Guard headquarters on his way to the officer's mess. *Another day down, another crisis averted.*

He smiled to himself. Wearying or not, he wouldn't choose any other life.

The lights cut out.

Fok, not again.

Before he had time to react, the lights returned at maximum output. He shielded his eyes from the sudden brightness.

Power surge? It was wishful thinking. No controls would have the illumination at those levels.

Kaen stepped over to the nearest information screen on the corridor wall, but he stopped in his tracks when he saw foreign code scrolling across the screen. His heart leaped into his throat. *We've been hacked.*

Orion Station's security had never been compromised—not on this level. If an enemy had gained control of the computer network, they could easily get physically inside the base.

Without hesitation, Kaen sprinted toward the corridor leading to the operational command center.

— — —

Leon powered down his workstation for the day, relieved to finally be finished with the most recent round of Gaelon sample testing.

"Team happy hour!" Tess exclaimed. "It's like we're bonding, or something."

"Calling attention to the fact kinda ruins the magic," Jack replied.

Leon smiled. He hadn't experienced proper team comradery since grad school on Mysar, and it felt good to be part of a group again.

"Kira will likely join us later on," he said. "So, Jack, try to keep the 'weird science experiment' talk to a minimum, okay?"

"Hey, I can conduct myself like a reasonable person. I mean, nanites aren't everything. There are recessive genetic traits to talk about, like her red hair," Jack replied.

Leon laughed. "Dude, you *really* don't want to go th—"

He stopped short when the lights turned off.

Instead of complete darkness like he expected, there was a subtle blue glow illuminating the lab.

The darkness lasted only a split second. When the lights returned, they were so bright, he had to squint.

"Did you see that glow?" he asked.

"Yeah, I did notice something," Tess concurred. "What was it?"

"Hit the switch." Leon instructed.

Jack, who was closest to the controls, turned off the

overhead lights.

There were a few low lights from ambient equipment, but a distinct blue glow was coming from elsewhere.

Leon looked around for the source of the light and was surprised to see it emanating from the rack containing the samples from Gaelon.

His brow knitted. "Uh, did they do that before?"

"Fok if I know!" Jack exclaimed. "But that doesn't look good."

Leon looked closer. "Wait, is that moving?"

The fragments were crawling up the sides of the test tubes and congregating near the stoppers. There was no mistaking that they were trying to burrow through.

"Shite, can it get out?" The panic was evident on Tess' face even in the low light cast from the glowing samples.

"Better question: what could it do if it *does* get out?" Jack asked.

Leon didn't want to find out.

"We need to get it in something more secure," he said, his mind racing about what that might be. He scanned around the room. "The glove box! Come on."

Leon raced toward the rack, grabbing a pair of tongs from a canister of tools on his way.

Jack grabbed another set of tongs while Tess opened the side of the glove box, a one-meter-wide transparent cube with built-in rubber gloves on two walls, which was used for handling potentially contaminated materials. It didn't come into play too often in their research activities, but the thick, corrosion-resistant walls stood the best chance of anything in the lab to contain the tiny particles.

Leon and Jack each grabbed test tubes with the tongs and gingerly transplanted them to the bottom of the glove box. Tess closed the hatches over the four glove openings as an extra precaution.

"Was this stuff alive the whole time?" she murmured.

"Depends on your definition of life," Leon replied while transporting another vial.

"Crawly, glowy things certainly seem to fit," Jack said. "Not that I'm crazy about the idea of a bunch of rock that had been exposed to the vacuum of space suddenly being able to spring into action like this."

"Is it too far a leap to hypothesize that it's connected to whatever is going on with the lights on the station?" Tess ventured.

"With this timing, no," Leon replied. He placed another test tube in the glove box; only three more to go.

Tess wilted. "That means it's…"

"Foking Trols," Jack completed for her.

"But computers!" Tess objected.

"They got one of the external processors," Jack reminded the two scientists. "If they're as good at reverse engineering as it seems like they are, then it's no surprise they figured out a hack."

"But where are they? Is this telepathic?" Tess' eyes were wide with worry and wonder.

Leon placed the final sample vial in the glove box, then swung the side hatch closed and latched it. "I have a feeling we're about to find out."

— — —

"Fokity fok," Kira said under her breath.

"Theory, Captain?" Sandren asked as he shielded his eyes from the overly bright lights.

"Weird happenings on both starships *and* at base?

Someone or something has hacked into our central control systems," Kira replied.

"I figured as much. Care to hazard a guess at whom?"

"I really want to be wrong, but I'd put money on the Trols taking advantage of the tech we inadvertently left them."

<I hate to concur, but I do,> Jasmine said in her mind. *<This is bad.>*

"Fantastic," Sandren said in a low voice, shaking his head. "We need to get to central command. If it's them, you're our best chance at opening a dialogue."

"Yes, sir."

They set off at a fast jog from Sandren's office, following the main corridors on a direct route to the control center at the heart of the star-shaped station. Other soldiers in the halls quickly moved out of their way. A few tried to ask questions, but the major ignored them all. Kira followed his lead.

A dozen meters from the control center entrance, Kira spotted Colonel Kaen approaching from the opposite direction.

"Sir," Kira acknowledged.

"Major, Captain," Kaen greeted with a curt nod. "It would seem we were due for another crisis."

"All to keep us on our toes, sir," Kira replied. She forced a smile, but on the inside she was terrified to find out what they were up against.

Kaen was the first through the entry door, followed by Sandren. Kira reluctantly followed.

The round room was abuzz with activity. Communications techs were yelling at each other across their consoles, arranged in two concentric circles, and officers were barking orders. Kira tuned out the din in an attempt to identify any information about what was going on. Nothing stood out, aside from a list of errors flashing in red on the broad viewscreen wrapping the back wall.

<Jasmine, you have anything?> she asked.

<Systems are down. We're locked out.>

<Can you get in?>

<Not alone,> Jasmine replied.

Kira stepped up next to Sandren, while Kaen ran over to talk with the other senior officers gathered in the center of the room.

"Sir, Jasmine said the controls are locked."

"I've never seen anything like this," Sandren murmured. "I thought we were dealing with a telepathic enemy, but this…"

"They don't just manipulate biology. Technology, too," she replied. "But I didn't see a computer hack coming, either. I'd really hoped they were all dead."

"Me too."

Kira looked around the room. "Until we can put a face to these things, I can't do anything here. But I do happen to know two of the best hackers around."

Sandren looked at her under his brow. "Hack our own computer network?"

"If we're locked out, what other choice do we have?"

"All right, get them up here," Sandren agreed.

<Jasmine, do you have access to communications?> Kira asked in her mind.

<No, everything *is locked. It's a small miracle we still have life support.>*

"I'll need to find them in person," Kira told Sandren. "I'll be back as soon as I can."

He nodded. "I'll relay your recommendation to the other officers. If it's a go, we'll be ready for you when you return with Kyle and Nia."

"Yes, sir."

Kira raced from the control room toward the corridor leading to the residential arm housing her team. She'd normally hop on the maglev, but with the power fluctuations, getting trapped in a transport car was too great a risk. Besides, with her new abilities, running was a breeze.

She tore past the confused soldiers traversing the halls in an attempt to find answers, deftly navigating the corridors until she reached the part of her trek where she needed to go vertically.

<I'm going to guess that taking the lift is a bad idea.>

<If you thought being trapped in a maglev car was bad, pretty sure an elevator is on a whole other level… literally.>

Kira rolled her eyes. *<Jasmine, that was terrible.>*

She reached the ladder access shaft, which was two meters from the main elevator bank. Twisting the lever to the side, she swung the hatch door open. She peeked inside. It was a long way up—nine stories to her destination.

<Keep my palms from sweating, will you?> Kira began her ascent.

<With your new grip strength, it won't matter.>

<All the same, falling to our death would be a lame way to go.>

She made quick time up the ladder and unbolted the access hatch on the destination level.

Her team's quarters were forty meters down the main corridor and off a short side passageway.

Please be here, Kira wished silently to herself. She knocked on the door.

To her relief, the bolt unlocked after five seconds, and the door opened a crack. Kyle peered back at her.

"Kira?" He swung the door open fully.

"Hey." She spotted Nia and Ari seated at the table. "Thank the stars you're here! We need you."

The soldiers came to attention.

"What's going on?" Nia asked.

"Pretty sure the Trols hacked into our central network," Kira stated.

"Foking external processor," Kyle swore.

"Yeah, I knew that was going to come back to bite our asses in a bad way," Kira said. "But beating ourselves up again won't help. Our immediate concern is we're locked out of our own systems."

"Shite, really?" Nia stood up.

"My crazy suggestion was for you two to try to hack in," Kira continued. "They're waiting for us back at the command hub."

Nia cast Kyle a look bordering on pure glee. "It's what we always dreamed of doing."

Kyle's eyes were bright with equal wonder. "The ultimate test of skill."

"Yeah, happy for you, and all, but this isn't for bragging rights," Kira stated.

"Oh, but there's going to be *so* much bragging," Kyle replied with a grin. He ran to the locker at the foot of his bunk to retrieve his equipment kit. "What are we waiting for? Let's go!"

"What should I do?" Ari asked from the table.

"Wait here. We don't need the muscle right now," Kira told him. "I'll be in touch as soon as we get the comms working again."

"Good luck," he replied.

Kira led Kyle and Nia back to the ladder she'd ascended.

"Ugh, I hate ladders," Nia commented as soon as she saw

the narrow chute.

"We use ladders *all the time*." Kyle climbed inside.

"That doesn't make me detest them any less!" she shot back while following him.

Kira groaned and waited for Nia to descend enough so she could enter. <*Sometimes, those two...*> she commented to Jasmine.

<*Geniuses always have their quirks.*>

<*Yet another thing to be careful saying around them. I made the mistake of calling Kyle 'brilliant' once. He spent the next week referring to himself as a 'demigod'.*> Kira began descending the ladder.

<*That seems like a bit of a leap.*>

<*If there is a leap to be made, they'll find a way.*>

<*Your team is very strange, Kira.*>

<*Not like I'm the image of normalcy myself.*>

Jasmine paused. <*That's a good point.*>

At the bottom of the ladder, Kira took the lead for the run back to the command hub. To her surprise, Kyle and Nia were more winded than her when they arrived.

"Wait here for a moment," she told them, both to give them an opportunity to catch their breath and so she could get final clearance on her hacking plan.

Kira entered the command room to find that the shouting had stopped. The near-silence was somehow more disconcerting.

She spotted Kaen and Sandren standing at the center of the room with the other senior officers, including General Lucian.

<*If this suggestion is going to get shot down, it will be in spectacular fashion,*> Kira said to Jasmine.

<*Even the highest commanders are still people,*> Jasmine pointed out.

People or not, it was still intimidating.

Kira gathered her courage and approached the group. "Sirs." She gave a differential nod.

General Lucian evaluated her. "I heard you want to try hacking our own computer network."

Kira met the general's level gaze. "Yes, sir. If the techs are unable to gain access through other means, maybe Kyle and Nia can help."

"So much for keeping those two out of trouble." He sighed. "I didn't think it'd come to it, but our other efforts have yet to yield results. Have them proceed. Just... try not to break anything."

"Yes, sir," Kira acknowledged. She saluted, then ran back to the hall to retrieve her team members.

"We're a go," she told them. "General Lucian said not to break anything."

"Psh, we always leave things more organized than we found them," Nia replied.

"Except when we really fok something up," Kyle whispered.

"Shh!" Kira lowered her voice. "Don't do that."

Kyle waved his hand. "I'm ninety-nine point seven percent sure we won't cause irreparable damage."

"It's that point three percent that worries me," Kira muttered. "I'll leave you to it."

She stood at a distance with her arms crossed while the two tech specialists got settled at adjacent workstations along the curved outer wall.

"Wow, they really did a number on the system," Nia muttered while she tried to gain access to the locked directories.

"This encryption pattern is familiar," Kyle mused.

"Definitely resembles what we encountered in Gaelon."

Kira's heart sank. *As if we didn't have enough evidence already that the Trols were back.*

<*Well, shite,*> she said to Jasmine.

<*You always suspected that there were more of them. This isn't a complete surprise.*> The AI caught herself. <*Well, the computer system hack is, but not the return of the Trols.*>

<*I can't help but feel like this is my fault.*> Kira groaned in her mind.

<*You have such a savior complex.*>

<*Yeah, well, I defeated them once and I can only imagine I'll be expected to do it again.*>

Jasmine laughed. <*You could desert—go find a tropical beach and hang out until this blows over.*>

<*And miss all the action? No way.*>

<*Yep, thought so. Save the day once and it goes to your head.*>

<*Doesn't help that you're in my head, egging me on,*> Kira shot back.

<*And you love it.*>

"Fok!" Nia exclaimed, returning Kira's attention to the events in front of her.

"What's wrong?" she asked.

"Our normal tricks aren't working," the soldier replied. "Just need to beat the system into submission, nothing to worry about."

"Maybe we should have brought Ari after all," Kira said in an attempt to lighten the mood.

Nia chuckled. "When in doubt, hit it with a hammer, right?"

"Or shoot it with a plasma rifle," Kyle added. "The glow of melting computer innards is rather beautiful."

Kira snickered to herself. She was always impressed by how the two could maintain witty banter while typing. Sometimes she thought it even made them work even better.

After several seconds of silence, Kyle sighed. "Remember when we were joking back in the Protheon facility about getting a real challenge? Well, we got it."

"But you can get in, right?" Kira asked cautiously. She'd never doubted her team's abilities in all their years working together. Five minutes tops, they could get into anything. The fact that they'd passed the seven minute mark was a testament to the severity of their present situation.

"Yeah, of co—" Kyle cleared his throat. "I think so."

<Fok, he has never *not had a firm 'yes' answer before,>* Kira said to Jasmine.

<I've been trying to help out, and it's a mess in there,> the AI replied. *<We're making progress, but the encryption keeps morphing. Two steps forward, one step back kind of thing.>*

<But you'll be able to get ahead of it?>

<Well, we have to before it gains complete control of the life support systems, don't we?>

Kira gulped. *<Sorry, I'll leave you to it.>*

Her concern deepened as the minutes passed. Even Kyle and Nia were relatively quiet, aside from the occasional comment or profane outburst.

Kira glanced over every so often at the officers in the center of the room, but their frowns prompted her to turn away. *Kyle and Nia will get this. They're the best.*

<All right, we're close,> Jasmine said in Kira's mind, breaking the relative silence. *<A dozen non-sentient AIs have been working with us to isolate the malicious code.>*

<Don't just isolate it—destroy it!>

<We will,> Jasmine assured her, *<but we're running a trace*

first to find out where it came from.>

As much as Kira didn't want bad news, they needed that information. The Trols had launched an assault on her home. That meant war.

"Communications are back online!" a comm tech announced from a workstation near the center of the room.

"So are environmental controls!" another tech called out.

A moment later, the lights returned to normal illumination levels, and the flickering on the control panels subsided.

"Status!" General Lucian demanded.

"No reports of damage to the station or personnel injuries," the comm tech continued. "All mechanical systems check out."

"Then what happened?" Kaen asked.

"It's a signal," Kyle chimed in. "Remote interference."

"One source broadcasting to Guard assets in this sector of Taran space," Nia added. "I've never seen anything quite like it."

General Lucian frowned. "What's the source?"

"It's originating beyond the border of Empire territory. The closest named system is… the Elvar Trinary," Kyle replied.

<Fok me,> Kira swore in her mind.

<It'll be okay,> Jasmine tried to soothe her. *<We'll stop them, just like last time.>*

"There's a scouting sensor array in the vicinity," Kyle continued.

"I can try to patch in a visual feed," the comm tech said. "Resolution won't be good at that range, though."

"Do it," Kaen instructed.

A minute passed while Kyle, Nia, and the comm tech tried to resolve the sensor data. Finally, the holographic display at the center of the room illuminated with the pixelated image of a sphere.

"What is it?" Kira asked no one in particular. "A probe?"

Kyle shook his head slowly. "No, a ship?"

Kaen paled. "What's the scale of this?"

"The diameter is seven thousand kilometers," the comm tech reported.

Kira nearly choked on her own breath. "That's the size of a planet!"

"Where the fok did it come from?" Kaen questioned. "How did we miss its approach? The gravity signature alone of something that size would have an effect on the surrounding systems."

"How in the stars does something that large move?" General Lucian added.

The comm tech worked her mouth. "There's no record of the object before fifteen minutes ago. I don't have an explanation. And... the space around it isn't reacting like it should around an object that size."

"Shite." Kaen turned away from the group of officers for a moment. He took a deep breath, then pivoted toward General Lucian. "How would you like to proceed, sir?"

"Send a scout ship on a recon mission. Let's get some intel on this beast."

CHAPTER 5

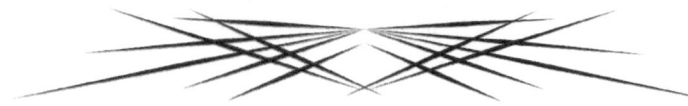

OF ALL THE foking things that could happen... Kaen jogged back to his office.

A reconnaissance ship had been deployed on an intercept course with the Trol planet-ship. They'd have more information soon, but in the meantime, Kaen's mind ran wild with the awful possibilities for what the Trols could do with a vessel that size.

He'd thought they were done with that particular race of foes—he'd needed them to be. The invasion of his mind was the most personal battle he'd ever had to fight, and knowing that there were more of the beings still out there, stronger than ever, resurfaced those terrible memories he'd tried to forget.

For all their resources, the Empire didn't have a ship on the same scale. That didn't mean their weapons weren't more powerful, but it did make Kaen wonder what else might be lurking out in the depths of space.

More than physical opposition, though, there was the question of the mind. Back when they'd first crossed paths with the Trols, it had appeared that specific neural pathways composed of valteron needed to be present in the brain to create a telepathic receptor, or TR. Only those who'd ingested the mineral and had the TR could be taken over remotely by the alien consciousness. However, in the assault on the Gaelon System, all Guard soldiers present—aside from Kira—had become paralyzed in a telepathic grip.

Based on that experience, it would seem the TR was necessary for long-distance telepathic control, but the Trols had the potential to exert some measure of control over anyone at close proximity. Any ship, any crew sent to intervene, might find itself incapacitated before they had a chance to act, if they got too close.

The obvious answer was to send a ship piloted by an AI, but with the revelation that the Trols could also now hack into the secure Guard network, a ship would likely suffer the same fate as a biological crew.

They have us cornered. Though Kaen hated to admit it, he couldn't ignore the reality. They were up against an opponent they didn't yet know how to fight.

But while they tried to find a weakness, there were people in immediate danger.

The alien planet-ship was three days away from the Elvar Trinary at its present velocity, and it would be visible on the system's long-range scan well before that. Kaen had no interest in finding out what would happen when it reached the system, but until they learned how to stop it, they needed to prepare for the worst-case scenario.

As soon as he reached his office, Kaen brought up the contact information for President Joris of Elusia. The computer warned Kaen that it was 02:00 local time in the Elusian capital city, but the conversation couldn't wait. He initiated the call.

Twenty seconds passed.

"Colonel?" President Joris answered over a voice-only connection.

"Sorry to contact you in the middle of your night, but it's urgent," Kaen replied. "We have a developing situation."

The president groaned. "What's going on?"

"The Trols are back," Kaen revealed. "This time, they have a ship headed toward the Elvar Trinary."

He breathed a sigh of relief. "A ship! I thought you were about to say they have an entire fleet."

"The ship is seven thousand kilometers in diameter."

Silence.

"H-How...?" Joris stammered at last.

"We don't know, but considering the ship is two-thirds the size of Elusia, I wanted to give you as much advance notice as possible," Kaen continued. "My best guess is that the vessel was emitting a signal to mask its presence while it made the approach—similar to the interference we observed in the Gaelon System. A dark patch on scan doesn't stand out unless you know to look for something."

"They could have been in transit for years, or..." Joris took a shaky breath. "What kind of offensive capabilities does the ship have?"

"I'll know more in a few hours. Don't worry, this is a top priority for the Guard, and we'll do everything in our power to keep your system safe."

"That's it? You wake me in the middle of the night to tell me a planet-sized ship is headed for us, but 'don't worry'?! How the fok am I—"

Kaen took a slow breath. "Mister President, would you rather it surprise you in another eighteen hours when it shows up on the long-range scans from your system's sensor array?"

"We're defenseless," Joris shot back. "How do you expect me to react?"

"I know this is a lot to process, but you're not facing this alone," Kaen said calmly. "Take a few hours to gather your thoughts. Your people will be looking to you for guidance, and I know you'll be able to lead them through this crisis. The Guard is already preparing a coordinated response."

Joris took a deep breath. "All right. Thank you."

"I'll be in touch as soon as I know more." Kaen ended the call.

As much he disliked emotional outbursts from those in positions of authority, Kaen didn't blame Joris. Were he in the president's position, he probably would have sworn a whole lot more.

— — —

Ellen awoke to an incessant chirp coming from the desk in the living room of her temporary apartment.

What time is it? She glanced at the clock on her nightstand and saw that it was 04:07. *Who would be calling me at this hour?*

The chirp was more annoying than usual, which she attributed to the hour. However, when she hauled herself out of bed to check the notification, she realized that the sharper tone was because the communication was flagged as high-priority.

It was coming from the Elusian capital, and it was only 02:07 there.

Shite! Ellen hurriedly wrapped a robe around herself, then answered the call.

President Joris appeared on her monitor, dark circles

under his eyes and hair unkempt. "I just spoke with Colonel Kaen," he said. "They've detected a Trol ship headed for our system."

Ellen's heart leaped into her throat. "What?!"

"I don't have any more information at this time, other than that it's huge—roughly the size of Mysar."

She shook her head, mystified. "That's…"

"I didn't want to believe it myself."

"We're completely foked," Ellen breathed. "Here we thought we defeated them, but that was just the warmup round so they could see what defenses we had to offer."

"That was my first impulse, too, but we can't give into that way of thinking. The colonel said not to worry, so the Guard must be working on a plan," Joris told her.

"So, what, we pretend everything is okay? I wish I didn't know." She smoothed back her light brown hair from her face. *What could we possibly do in defense? If we evacuate everyone, where would we go?*

A vise tightened around her heart. No, there wouldn't be an evacuation; there weren't enough ships in the system to transport all the citizens. They were trapped on their worlds, subject to whatever horrific fate the Trols had planned.

President Joris straightened in his seat. "Someone on Mysar needed to be informed, and you're the closest thing the world has to a leader right now."

"I'm not—"

"Ellen, I need you to keep a level head. I've seen you under pressure before. You can do this."

She took two slow breaths and nodded. "Yes, sir."

"Now. I don't know what the Guard is planning, but I wanted to give you a heads up so that you would have time to process the situation. When we get our directions, we'll need to be a calm presence of authority above the inevitable chaos."

"What about Valta?" Ellen asked.

"Do you know Mitchell Korwen?"

"Not personally, but he's been Tribeca's mayor since I was a teenager," Ellen replied. "If you're asking if he would be a good point of contact, then yes."

Joris nodded. "I'll reach out to him."

"How long before the ship is visible on scan?"

"Less than eighteen hours. It will arrive in three days."

Ellen swallowed. "Okay. Let's hope the Guard has their plan before then."

— — —

"A giant foking planet-ship," Kira muttered. "These Trol bastards must have some kind of inferiority complex with a constant need to overcompensate for their nanoscopic size."

Across the conference table, Leon and Sandren chuckled, but Kaen looked decidedly less amused.

"We're looking for actionable theories," the colonel stated.

"Sorry, sir." Kira looked down.

"It *is* pertinent to note the scale of the vessel," Sandren began. "Its sheer enormity says a lot about its potential use."

"That's a good point," Kaen agreed. "Something planet-sized is probably dealing with planet-scale concerns, rather than any matter involving an individual."

"Yes, but we can't rule out an individual-scale component," Kira said. "Based on what we observed in Gaelon, it's possible that this ship might also contain a soldier factory."

Kaen gave a grim nod. "But with this ship, they could abduct the entire population of a planet."

"Stars! The Elvar Trinary has so few full-time residents that they could abduct everyone in the whole system," Kira said without thinking, only to immediately realize that those weren't faceless victims—they were her friends and family.

Leon exchanged glances with her, clearly realizing the same thing. "For that matter," he said, "this structure isn't bound to surface area in the same way that a planet is. Looking at the volume potential of the structure, it could reasonably hold the population of dozens of systems."

"Or the entire thing could be a mega-weapon," Kira countered.

"Whatever it is, it was able to interface with the station and Guard ships," Leon said. "It also activated the debris we collected from the Gaelon System."

"What do you mean?" Kaen asked.

"The dust was glowing… and moving around in the vials. It wasn't able to get out, but it definitely wanted to do something other than sit in a test tube."

The colonel frowned. "What's going on with it now?"

"It went dormant again as soon as you got control of the computer system," Leon replied.

"Hmm." Kira crossed her arms. "You think that has anything to do with the flickering monitors? I wonder if the hack caused the computer equipment to emit a signal that activated it."

Leon nodded. "A reasonable hypothesis."

"And the source of that signal is this new ship, I presume?" Sandren said.

"The ship's appearance and the impact on the Guard fleet would suggest as much," Kaen replied. "But there's more to this ship than a transmitter, and it falls to us to determine the potential function of the vessel. The engineering report from the survey ship highlighted some key components that may offer clues." Kaen adjusted the three-dimensional holoprojection of the spherical ship floating above the center of the table.

Eight circular recesses highlighted around the sphere's equator, then the view zoomed in on one to show it as a cross-section. The apparent circle was actually a cylinder.

Kira tilted her head. "That's... weird."

"The mechanical components suggest that these cylinders can extend outward," Sandren observed. "There are slots ringing each."

Indeed there were. Kira tried to count them but quickly lost track.

<Seventy-two in each,> Jasmine supplied for her.

<That's a lot of... whatever those things are.>

Across the table, Leon was scowling at the holographic projection. "I can't wrap my head around this scale. I keep thinking it's something manageable, but those cylinders are a hundred kilometers apart, and each slot is a kilometer long. It's *huge*."

Sandren shook his head. " 'Mind-boggling' would be an understatement."

Wait a minute... Kira did a double-take at the model. *<Hey, Jasmine, we've encountered a kilometer-long cylinder recently, haven't we?>*

<You don't mean the pits on Gaelon and Mysar, do you?>

<That's exactly what I was thinking.>

<Maybe,> the AI agreed. *<Go ahead. It's your idea to bring up.>*

<You think it's stupid.>

<No, I think it fits surprisingly well. I just don't like the implications.>

Kira cleared her throat. "So, um, crazy idea... What if each of the slots in those giant cylinders were to hold a pit like the ones in Gaelon and Mysar? Eight around and nine deep."

Leon slumped in his chair. "Fok."

Kaen spread his hands on the tabletop. "What makes you suggest that, Kira?"

"Nothing aside from scale, sir," she replied. "We observed two structures approximately one kilometer deep with an interior diameter of ten meters, and this thing happens to have slots one kilometer long and thirty meters wide. You asked for ideas, and mine is that that contraption is a giant core sampler. I don't know if it inserts the pits or takes them out, but there you have it."

Sandren did the math. "If they only need one per system to get a foothold, then…"

"Our little happy corner of the galaxy is in trouble if that ship is left unchecked," Kira completed when he trailed off.

"If I may add," Jasmine said over the audible comms, "these cores—if that is, indeed, what they are—make up only a fraction of the ship's function."

Kaen nodded, bringing up a different set of highlighted plans.

This version of the holographic model focused on a series of short towers ringing a single, tall tower. Four protrusions around the central grouping looked to be folded mechanical arms, but the exact nature and purpose were unclear.

"I've got nothing," Kira said.

"If there was one component of this ship for population transport, we can assume there would need to be a means to craft a new home," Jasmine continued over the comm. "I've run this configuration through the Guard database, and it is most likely some form of weapon."

"A weapon that's six hundred kilometers in diameter?

That's not…" Kaen faded out.

"The scale doesn't change my assessment of the information at my disposal. That said, my specialty is in biomedical applications, not military weaponry."

"Same here," Leon said. "I'm a—"

"Geneticist, we know," Kaen cut him off. "But the people sitting in this room are the resident Trol experts, regardless of our backgrounds. For better or worse, our hunches related to these guys have a good track record of being correct. If Jasmine thinks this is a weapon, then I'm inclined to proceed accordingly. And, assuming it is, it's not just a planet-killer—it's a system-killer."

"To what end?" Kira threw up her hands.

"Raw materials," Leon murmured. He sat upright in his chair, chuckling to himself. "Of course."

"Care to enlighten us?" Kaen prompted.

"All of their structures are manufactured, right? That requires raw materials. Mining raw materials is highly time- and labor-intensive. It's way easier to smash a target to bits, scoop it up, and sort through the matter after the fact."

"A weapon to blast worlds apart, then a processing plant, or whatever, to extract the useful materials?" Kira clarified.

"Something like that," Leon replied. "But it's a guess."

"I agree with the assessment," Jasmine stated over the comm.

Kira groaned. "Problem is, that next 'target' is Leon's and my home system."

Leon's face flushed. "I'd kinda like to keep it from getting destroyed, if we can."

"Agreed." Kira looked over the holographic ship. "So, how do we stop this thing?"

CHAPTER 6

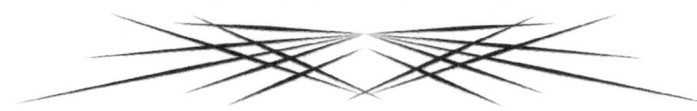

KAEN LOOKED GENERAL Lucian in his eyes. "This is too big a threat for the Guard to handle alone. We need to involve the TSS."

The general nodded. "I agree. I've briefed the TSS High Commander, and the *Conquest* is en route."

"That's excellent news, sir." If that ship couldn't contain the Trol vessel, it was unlikely anything else in the Guard or Tararian Selective Services' fleet stood much of a chance. Kaen has seen footage of the TSS *Conquest*'s legendary telekinetic weapon used in the Bakzen War, but witnessing it in person would be a sight to behold. Moreover, he would finally meet a TSS Agent in person—no doubt, one of their most powerful.

"A word of caution," General Lucian continued. "I've met the ship's captain before. It was not a pleasant exchange."

"Sir?"

The general seemed to search for the right words. "His gifts have made him arrogant. It doesn't help that he's the High Commander's son."

Kaen came to attention. "You mean, he's…"

It had become common knowledge in recent years that the Sietinen Dynasty had a hand in many Taran affairs. A longstanding and respected High Dynasty, the family was the first to openly display telekinetic Gifts—an affront to the Priesthood at the time. Cris Sietinen had assumed the position as Head of the Sietinen Dynasty, and his son, Wil, served as TSS High Commander. Given Wil's acclaim as a hero of the Bakzen War, it stood to reason that a child of his would be highly capable. Even while acting as an Agent of the TSS, that didn't change the fact that the *Conquest*'s captain was veritable Taran royalty.

"The TSS has always made it a point to separate birthright from an individual's station within the organization. I'm not sure if Jason Sietinen sees things that way, but I advise you to think of him as a TSS Agent and nothing more," General Lucian said.

"Yes, sir," Kaen acknowledged.

He wasn't one to get wrapped up in celebrity, but the Sietinens were the most famous family in the entire Taran sphere. *Anyone would get a little awe-struck. I wonder what happened between Jason and General Lucian?* Given the general's reticence on the matter, Kaen figured it was better not to ask.

"The *Conquest* will be waiting for you at Redstar Station," Lucian instructed.

"I'll arrange transport right away. Also, sir, I suggest that Kira Elsar accompany me—in the event we're able to make telepathic contact."

The general nodded. "This may be our only chance to learn more about them. Good luck."

— — —

Kira lay on her bed next to Leon, staring up at the ceiling. "It's just so stupid-big."

"I know, I can't fathom it, either." He sighed.

"I don't understand how that thing could move around," she continued. "I mean, it didn't have any visible engines."

"Beats me."

"Maybe it uses subspace in some way?"

"We do know that they use telepathy through a subspace link, so it's possible." Leon agreed.

"Stars, I really wish we didn't have to deal with this right now." She shook her head.

"I know, but you'll figure out a way to beat them, just like you did before."

Kira appreciated the confidence in his tone, but she couldn't quite muster up the same level of enthusiasm. The last encounter with the Trols had taken a lot out of her, and she wasn't eager to go through the experience again—let alone with an even bigger, meaner-looking base of operations.

"Thank you for always believing in me," she said after a pause.

"Always." Leon took her hand.

"Even Colonel Kaen was worried. I don't think I've seen that before."

"It is a pretty tense situation. I don't envy those in charge."

Kira repositioned to rest her head on his shoulder. "They're going to look to me for a solution. I don't know if I'll be able to do what I did last time."

"Sure you will."

"I dunno, maybe. But I don't want to. I had to go to this dark place in myself—fueled by an anger and bitterness that's not truly a part of me."

Leon swiveled to look at her. "That wasn't all of it, from what you told me."

"Love and happiness? That's never triggered a transformation for me."

"You've also never tried."

She let out a heavy sigh. "I guess it's time I embrace this change and start having it work for me, rather than the other way around."

"Now, that's the kind of attitude that I'd expect to get results."

"You're pretty good at these pep-talks."

"If only the ones I gave *myself* worked half as well."

Kira was about to reply when the comm chirped with an incoming communication. She sat up to check the screen set into the wall next to the door; it was from Colonel Kaen.

She held up her finger for Leon to hold this thought, then accepted the voice call. "Colonel."

"Kira, the TSS has agreed to a joint op. We'll use the *Conquest*'s TK weapon against the Trol ship. Before we resort to those extremes, however, I'd like to make one final attempt at contact. Meet me at Berth 17 for immediate departure."

"Yes, sir. I'm on my way." She cast a wide-eyed look of surprise at Leon.

"See you soon." Kaen ended the call.

"The *Conquest*? Holy shite." Kira whistled.

"Fancy?" Leon asked.

"*Very* fancy. Didn't you hear about its use in the Bakzen War?"

"Can't say I ever read much about Taran military history. The Elvar Trinary was removed from all of that."

"Well, suffice to say it's a super-fok-up-the-bad-guys kind

of ship, if anything in the historical records is correct."

Leon smiled. "Sounds like your kind of starship."

She grinned back. "Doesn't it? Man, my team is going to be so envious they don't get to see the action firsthand."

"I'll be sure to document the events for their review," Jasmine said over the room comm.

"Not the same, but it will have to do." Kira caught herself. "Shite! I need to pack." She jumped off the bed, running to her dresser to retrieve some undergarments for the trip.

Leon sat up and swung his legs over the side of the bed. "I know I don't need to say it, but—"

"I'll be careful." She gave him a quick kiss. "Should only be observation, and maybe a telepathic, 'You guys suck'."

"I hope it is that straightforward. It'd be nice to put these guys squarely in the past."

"Agreed." Kira grabbed a spare shipsuit and shoved it in her travel bag.

<*Toothbrush,*> Jasmine reminded her.

<*Right, thanks.*> Kira dashed into the bathroom to retrieve her toiletry bag.

Once it was stowed, she did a quick mental inventory. "Okay, that should be everything."

<*Check,*> Jasmine confirmed.

"I'll see you in a couple of days," she said to Leon, giving him a parting kiss, slow and deep. "Stay out of trouble."

"That's my line!" He smirked.

They exited her quarters. After another quick kiss, she jogged toward the designated berth for the transport ship.

Kaen was already on board and running through the pre-flight checks when she arrived at the vessel. She almost laughed out loud when she saw it was the *Lisbeth II*—the same vessel Kaen had commandeered while under Nox's influence a month prior.

"Hello, sir," she greeted. "Didn't think I'd find myself on this craft again."

"Welcome aboard," Kaen replied. "When I saw it was available, I couldn't resist. I feel like I owe the ship an apology, after what happened last time."

"I understand the sentiment." Kira stowed her travel bag in a cubby at the back of the cockpit.

"Besides, we won't need it for long. Just a quick hop to Redstar Station, and then we'll board the *Conquest*."

She took a seat in the co-pilot's chair. "Thank you for inviting me along. I've always wondered what the TSS ships are like."

Kaen flashed a rare smile. "Me too, for what it's worth."

He finished the pre-flight checks and then undocked the vessel from its umbilical—properly, unlike Kira's daring flight through the vacuum in her emergency suit. She had to say, this journey was off to a much better start.

The ship glided through the black to get far enough from Orion Station to initiate a jump. After making the transition to subspace, minutes dragged on in silence while they stared at the ethereal blue-green light surrounding the ship.

<Am I supposed to make small-talk?> Kira asked Jasmine.

<That's up to you. It's not like there's a particular Guard policy written for this exact situation.>

<This is so awkward. The last time we were on this ship together, I had him shackled to the floor and he was snarling at me.>

Jasmine laughed.

<Not helpful,> Kira groaned in her mind.

<Sorry. Picturing him snarling on the floor conjured an amusing image.>

<He was having a pretty bad day.>

<Certainly sounds like it.>

<But, seriously, do I just sit here in silence? How long will this jump take?> Kira asked the AI.

<One hour and three minutes remain until the estimated arrival time.>

Kira sighed inwardly. *<Yeah, that's way too long to sit here without saying anything. I think? Gah, I don't know.>*

<If you want to talk, then talk.>

<But he's the colonel.>

<You're acting like you've never had to make friendly conversation with a superior officer before.>

<Not one I once shackled to the floor! Or whose mind I dug around in.>

<Admittedly, the dynamic is not ideal,> Jasmine concurred. *<Just talk to him, Kira. You're overthinking it.>*

<Ugh, fine.>

She took a deep breath. "So, sir, how have you been since we removed Nox from your head?"

<Smooth, Kira. Way to ease into it with a light topic.>

Kaen looked taken aback for a moment and then smiled slightly. "You know, it's refreshing for someone to just come out and ask. Most try to dance around it."

"Sorry, I—"

"Don't apologize, it's a fair question. I've been happy to be myself again, but I've had a lot of reflecting to do on what occurred while I was under Nox's influence. You, of all people, understand what it means to be directed by a mind that's not your own."

She looked down. "I do often think about what it's like afterward, for people I've controlled. Most aren't a true enemy, just someone working for the wrong side."

He nodded. "That's a burden we carry as Guard soldiers. We fight for justice and try to determine the moral right, but there are still multiple sides to any conflict. You have the makings of a true officer, with your disposition to see that our truth is not absolute. What we perceive to be the correct path might be someone else's worst nightmare."

"It's amazing to think about how perspective can change so much. When I was younger and getting ready to leave Valta, it seemed so clear."

"Youth has a way of making things more black and white. By the time you get to my age, it's all shades of gray." He chuckled. "In fact, I think that's the real test of maturity, regardless of chronological age. When you can place yourself in the position of another person, with views opposite your own, and understand their feelings and motivations—only then are you truly ready to lead people on your own side."

"I guess I got a leg up with that, being able to *actually* be in someone else's mind," Kira realized.

"You did, but you've also paid attention and learned from the experience. I knew another telepath once, years ago—a civilian who'd occasionally contract with the Guard. Not as powerful as you, but he could glean the thoughts of others in a general sense, and also sense emotions in a way that made him excellent at detecting lies. He must have interrogated more than a hundred people by the time I met him. I once asked him if he'd noticed any trends in those interviews, and the only thing he had to say was, 'When you have a person cornered, they're only in it for themselves.' I thought that was one of the saddest things I'd ever heard—that that's all he took away."

Kira leaned back in her seat. "Wow, that *is* bleak. And I have to say, I disagree with his assessment."

"What's your experience been?"

"Venturing inside someone's mind is intimate. Sometimes I see the things that they don't want to readily admit to themselves. In some cases, the person never wanted to be in the position they're in—whether it be because of crappy job prospects, a familial obligation, or even forced servitude. Those people bend easily when I request information from them. They were never invested in keeping the secret, so they give it up without much of a fight."

"Is lack of conviction an excuse to abandon duty?" Kaen questioned.

"No, sir, I didn't mean to suggest—"

"I'm only asking as a thought exercise," he hastily added. "One officer to another."

Kira tapped her index finger on the seat's armrest. "Well, to that end, I guess I'd argue that you can't have complete loyalty without belief."

The colonel nodded. "The difference between having a job versus a career."

"Yeah, exactly. Unlike the people who'll cave at the first sign of pressure, there are also true believers," she continued. "Anyone of genuine conviction will stand by their mission and the greater purpose. Those are the people where I really have to dig, and they'll fight me every step of the way. When someone is convinced that their mission is the only right way, they will do everything within their power to see it through."

"Those are the kind of people we try to cultivate in the Guard."

"And it shows," Kira agreed. "I've never questioned that anyone here has doubts about the work we're doing."

"Except those moments when one wonders if the career is what they were meant to do."

The statement caught Kira off-guard. "Sir!"

Kaen smiled. "I've been there, too, Kira. That decade mark is a funny thing—makes you wonder how many different directions your life could have gone, had you made other choices."

"I want to be here, sir."

"I know you do. But I also recognize that look you got in your eyes when you learned that your home system was in danger. As loyal as you are to the Guard and as much as you have made it your life, you can never sever your allegiance to your home—not completely."

"These recent missions have affected me in a way I didn't expect," she admitted.

"Not to mention a new companion, offering even greater reminders of those times past," Kaen added.

Kira's brows drew together. "I would never allow my relationship with Leon to compromise my performance as an officer."

"I didn't mean to imply that it would. In fact, I think it's those kinds of personal ties that make a person work even harder. It's people that have no love, no home, nothing bigger than themselves, that concern me. When someone is *really* only in it for themselves—*that's* cause for worry."

"So, that telepath you knew, was he only interrogating those kinds of people?" Kira asked.

"Stars, maybe he was. But I still think it's sad that he generalized those impressions and applied them to everyone."

"I agree, but..." Kira faded out, second-guessing her thought.

Kaen raised a questioning eyebrow.

"Well," she continued, "I was going to say that telepathic reading isn't an exact science. It's actually quite subjective. As much as I try to get a clear, accurate impression, I can't help getting some overlay of my own emotions."

"Makes sense."

"So, with a person like your old friend, I can't help but wonder if it was *him* who was dissatisfied with his work—that his bleak view of other's people's motivations stemmed from having no passion or conviction in his own life."

"An astute observation," Kaen replied. "A month after we met, he up and left one day, no explanation. None of us ever heard from him again."

"Wow."

"I like to think he did eventually find something fulfilling in his life. What he was doing certainly wasn't it."

Kira nodded. "I can see how working as an interrogator could bring a person to the edge. You *can't* only be in it for yourself."

"No, you can't." Kaen smiled. "I'm glad that Leon came back into your life when he did. It's funny how the universe has a way of delivering what we need, even when we don't yet realize anything was missing."

CHAPTER 7

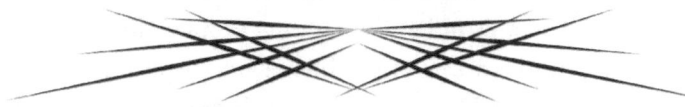

KIRA AND THE colonel made small-talk over the next hour on their journey to Redstar Station.

Kaen opened up more than Kira had ever witnessed, including accounts of his time as a Guard grunt during the Bakzen War. The effort had been led by the TSS, so the Guard was little more than a civil police force at the time.

Such tales always reminded Kira how young she was compared to some of her colleagues. It was only her unique telepathic skills that had placed her on an accelerated career path. Not that telepathy was everything, but being able to read minds and control people's actions did have its perks.

The *Lisbeth II* dropped out of subspace at Redstar Station in the Delphos System. At the intersection of several major transit routes through the sector, the station was a convenient hub for transit to almost anywhere in Taran space. Kira hadn't spent much time on the station itself, but its reputation as a gathering place for all sorts was widely known.

After docking, they gathered their travel bags and then

wove through the pedestrian traffic to the docking location of the *Conquest*. Viewports on the outer wall of the concourse provided the first glimpse of the vessel as they approached.

"Holy shite," Kira whispered as she took it in.

Though significantly smaller than the Guard's dreadnoughts, the *Conquest* lived up to its infamous reputation, with sleek lines that managed to be both breathtaking and menacing. The hull had a unique iridescence to it, like all TSS ships, which lent perfectly to the tapered, sculptural shape of the vessel. The most distinctive feature, however, was an ateron band wrapping around the perimeter of the ship from nose to aft, which Kira suspected was the energy relay for the TK weapon. Considering that they had a planet-sized problem, the super-weapon was the correct tool for the job.

"Have you ever had command of a joint op with the TSS before, sir?" Kira asked while they approached the gangway.

"No. But, between us, I always wanted to." His eyes were bright with the kind of excitement a child might display before receiving a long-awaited birthday present.

Were it anyone else, Kira might have mistaken his enthusiasm for being power-hungry. Having glimpsed inside Kaen's mind, though, she had no doubt that this was a dream come true for him—a career aspiration finally come to fruition, even if only for a few hours.

"I can't say I'd want the responsibility of being in command of a ship this size," Kira replied.

"I wouldn't want a command full-time," Kaen agreed, "but I don't think anyone who works for a space fleet hasn't fantasized at least once about captaining a ship for a day."

She smiled back. "All right, you have me there."

In Kira's case, her fantasy had begun at the age of seven. At the time, her fantasy ship had been purple and included a cocobera petting zoo. She had never shared that with a soul, and she wasn't about to start now—especially with Ari on the prowl for new blackmail material, after her stunt the prior month.

At the top of the gangway, a sentry was standing guard, dressed in the dark gray uniform of the TSS Militia—the non-Agent division of the organization.

"Colonel Terence Kaen and Captain Kira Elsar, reporting for duty," Kaen stated.

The sentry saluted. "The captain is expecting you, sir. The Command Center is to your right."

Kaen and Kira saluted back and then headed in the direction the sentry had specified.

The interior was a significant step up from the furnishings on the *Raven*, though still utilitarian by TSS standards, based on what Kira had heard of their equipment. Viewscreens placed in intervals along the length of the corridor depicted starscapes, complementing the warm-hued lights inset in the ceiling. They stopped at the open door to the ship's Command Center.

Kira's jaw dropped when she saw the design through the open doorway.

A transparent platform extended from the entry door into the center of the spherical room. Five bar-height black seats were arranged in the center of the main platform, with four around the perimeter and one at the center. Two control consoles faced outward at the front of the Commander Center a step down from the central platform. The entire room was wrapped in a continuous, spherical viewscreen with holographic augmentations, displaying the surroundings of the *Conquest*.

The control consoles were occupied by Militia officers, and a single TSS Agent stood next to the central command chair—recognizable by his all-black uniform with knee-length coat.

The Agent turned to evaluate them with his bioluminescent teal eyes, complementing chestnut hair. He was much younger than Kira expected—no more than early- or -mid-twenties—and strikingly good-looking. Kira had heard about a magnetic quality to TSS Agents, and he certainly had it in spades.

"Welcome aboard the TSS *Conquest*," he greeted, cracking a smile.

"Sir." Kaen strode into the Command Center, and Kira followed. "I'm Colonel Kaen, and this is Captain Elsar."

The Agent turned his attention to Kira. "The Captain Elsar from the Gaelon incident?"

"You heard about that?" Kira asked, surprised.

"You destroyed a dwarf planet using only your mind. News about that sort of thing gets around—especially considering you're not in the TSS."

Kira blushed. "Oh."

<*Why didn't you mention people were talking about me?*> Kira asked her AI.

<*You didn't ask, and you also seemed distracted enough as it was. You didn't think that no one would take notice, did you?*>

The private exchange was suddenly interrupted by a powerful presence. "*I was fascinated to learn about Valtan telepaths,*" the Agent said—stronger, even, than what Kira had experienced with the Trols. There was warmth and assurance to his mental projection, unlike the aliens' blind thirst for power. "*Why did you choose the Guard over the TSS?*"

"*I was rejected from the Agent track, and the Guard had more advancement potential than TSS Militia,*" Kira replied.

The exchange was faster than any telepathy she'd ever experienced—taking only a fraction of a moment to convey the thoughts.

"That may be worth revisiting," the Agent said, then severed the connection. He turned his palm upward in the Taran custom for greeting new acquaintances. "I'm Jason Sietinen. It's a pleasure to meet you."

Kira did a double-take. *<Did he just say Sietinen?>* she asked Jasmine.

<That's definitely him,> the AI confirmed.

"Sir, um…" Words failed her.

"Please, call me Jason," he said. "There have been too many Agent Sietinens to differentiate."

"Kaen will do for me," the colonel said.

"Kira works," she said. "I've always preferred first names with my own team."

Jason smiled. "Maybe that comes from being acquainted with others' minds. The TSS has never been much for formality."

"I imagine that was particularly interesting growing up in your family," Kaen commented.

"Actually, my sister and I grew up on Earth," Jason revealed.

The colonel nodded. "Ah, that's how the Sietinen heirs avoided the spotlight for so many years."

"Came as quite a shock when we were brought into the Taran fold at sixteen—especially finding out about our lineage. Raena clearly took more readily to it than I did."

Kira shrugged. "You have command of the *Conquest*. That seems to be embracing it, from where I stand."

He chuckled. "Yeah, I guess so. But considering TSS Headquarters' proximity to Earth, I haven't ventured far from home."

"I know what it's like to come from a world outside the core Taran society," Kira said. "You always have ties to home in one way or another."

Jason turned serious. "The Elvar Trinary has the backing of the Taran Empire. We'll eliminate this threat. Trust me— we've faced worse."

"Don't underestimate the Trols," Kira warned.

"Never," Jason assured her. "Whatever they can throw at us, I'm confident, with our combined resources, we'll come out on top."

"Very much looking forward to working with you," Kaen said.

"Likewise. I've never understood the distinction between the Guard and TSS," the young Agent said.

"Remnants from times past," Kaen mused.

Jason nodded. "I suspect so. More changes are coming in the near future, I can only imagine."

<He would know,> Kira commented to Jasmine.

<Few individuals are at the intersection of so many influencers. I didn't expect him to be so casual about his position.>

<Me either. Maybe that's from growing up on Earth.>

<Perhaps,> the AI agreed. <Now that I'm looking through the data archives, it appears that defying societal expectations is a trait of the Sietinens. His mother was also born and raised on Earth.>

<So, he probably understands how I feel about the Elvar Trinary.>

<It would seem so. Someone in his position is a powerful ally. That's a friendship worth cultivating.>

Kira mentally rolled her eyes. <I'm here for a mission

against the Trols, Jasmine—not politicking.>

<Suit yourself.>

Kira returned her attention to the goings-on in the Command Center. Kaen had apparently just asked about their flight plan.

"Transit time to intercept is five hours," Jason was saying. "You're welcome to get settled in while we get underway."

"Only five hours?" Kaen asked. "It's much further than that from the closest navigation beacon."

Jason gave him a quizzical look. "The Guard's ships aren't equipped with independent jump drives?"

"With what?" Kira questioned.

The Agent let out a long breath. "We aren't reliant on the SiNavTech beacon network to jump. I thought the new tech had been rolled out on a wider scale."

Kaen frowned. "I've heard of independent jump drives, but the Guard doesn't have any ships with those nav consoles, to my knowledge."

"All the more reason for us to start working together, I guess," Jason said with a shrug. "Anyway, we've set aside quarters for you, if you'd like to rest on the way over."

Kira looked down at her travel bag in hand. She was coming up on a full day without sleep, and the prospect was tempting.

Kaen picked up on her cue. "You go on, Captain," he said.

"Thank you, sir. I'll see you when we arrive." Kira nodded to the two commanders and then turned to go.

"I was wondering if I might get a tour of the ship..." Kaen asked while Kira was on her way out.

<Bomax! Just my luck I'd miss out on a tour,> she said to Jasmine.

<There will be plenty of time for that later,> the AI replied.

<Rest is the priority now.>

<No argument here.> Considering what they'd be up against when they arrived at their destination, Kira needed to be as sharp as possible.

CHAPTER 8

BETWEEN A TOUR of the *Conquest*, a nap, and his general excitement, the five hours of transit time flew by for Kaen.

As they made the final approach for the intercept with the Trol ship, Kaen settled into one of the ancillary seats at the center of the Command Center, with Jason in the center and Kira to his left. Kira still seemed mystified about being at the center of the action, but Kaen couldn't imagine having anyone else along. If the op went sideways, he wanted to have the one person who'd ever initiated contact with the Trols at his side.

A front section of the wraparound viewscreen was set to a magnified image of the void ahead. At the limits of visual range, a dull, spherical mass was coming into view. With minimal light of its own and no stars nearby, the sphere would be almost invisible, were it not for the enhancements offered by the holographic overlay.

"Well, it doesn't look so bad from this distance," Kira quipped.

Jason didn't look convinced. "Wait until we're right up

next to it."

"I have no intention of getting that close, after what happened to the fleet in Gaelon," Kaen stated. "Captain Elsar, see if you can make contact."

"We're kind of far out, sir," she replied. "But I'll try."

Kira focused ahead at the image of the Trol ship, getting a faraway look in her eyes.

It's amazing how she can do those things, Kaen thought from the seat next to her. *We'd be lost right now if it wasn't for her.*

Jason sat quietly, gazing at the image out the viewscreen while Kira set about her task.

After a minute of intense concentration, Kira's attention returned to the inside of the Command Center. "I dunno, sir, it's weird."

"Can you be more specific?"

"Eh." Kira frowned at the image of the Trol ship. "I didn't exactly get through to them, but it wasn't a lack of contact, either. The easiest way to describe it is that they were ignoring me. But… the presence wasn't like I experienced before, on Gaelon."

Kaen's brow knitted. "What do you mean?"

"There were more of them." She shook her head. "No, that's not the right way to put it. Communicating with Reya or Nox was like talking with a single presence. The contact on Gaelon was like hearing a chorus—distinct voices speaking together. But this ship here… it's like there are layers. I guess the best analogy would be a song. They were contributing to the same piece of music, but playing different parts in the harmony. Players, instrument groups, sections, all adding up to one orchestra. Only it was out of tune."

"In that case, is there a conductor?" Kaen asked.

"Not that I've been able to identify. Everything I've observed indicates that they're falling into whatever role is necessary. Even though there are individual minds, they work together as one, which means they must have some sort of governance. We saw that central column thing in Gaelon, so I can only imagine this mammoth thing has something like that, too. Target that regulating hub, and the orchestra won't know what song they're supposed to be playing."

"What do you think?" Kaen asked Jason, remembering it important to acknowledge there was another powerful telepath on board.

The young man crossed his arms. "I can glean a sense of what Kira is talking about, but the form of telepathy these beings use is unlike anything I've encountered before. Since Kira has an established rapport with them—friendly or not—I'm inclined to have her take the lead."

"Um, all right…" Kira said hesitantly.

Kaen didn't blame her for being a little shocked that a senior TSS Agent would be deferring to her for such matters, but it remained that Kira's abilities were uniquely suited for this particular situation. As long as he had his way, Kaen would prefer Kira handle the telepathic matters and just let Jason control the ship's TK weapon—if and when it came time to use it.

If there's a way to get through to them and open a dialogue, this is a chance to learn about a fascinating culture unlike any other, Kaen thought to himself.

He caught Kira's gaze, bidding her to open a private telepathic link.

"*Sir?*" she questioned in his mind.

"*Is there any chance of making meaningful contact? Do they just need time to warm up to you?*"

"*My honest assessment, sir, is that they think we're a lower lifeform unworthy of their attention. I don't think any amount of outreach will make a difference,*" Kira replied in his mind. "*I'm also painfully aware of the ticking clock while this system-killer ship marches toward my homeworld.*"

"*We won't let it get there.*" Kaen severed the connection.

"We're coming into attack range," a Militia officer, who'd been introduced as Rianne, offered from her station at the front of the Command Center.

The spherical target took up half the front viewing area without artificial magnification. They were twice as far back as the Guard fleet had been from the dwarf planet in Gaelon; Kaen hoped it was far enough.

Jason admired the sight. "Real aliens… this is the kind of thing we'd watch movies about when I was growing up."

"I assure you this is very real," Kaen stated.

"No doubt. It's a shame that our first contact with these beings has been so adversarial," he replied.

"They're still ignoring my attempts to make contact," Kira said.

Jason pursed his lips. "I can't get through, either."

"It sounds like they don't want to talk. I recommend we take them out while we have the opportunity," Kaen stated.

Jason inclined his head. "That is what we came here to do." A narrow pedestal rose from the deck in front of him, topped with two metal handholds. When it was at the appropriate height, he gripped the cylinders. "Now I know how my father felt." He didn't elaborate.

Stars, let this be the right move. Kaen nodded. "Proceed."

The TSS Agent focused on the image of the sphere on the viewscreen. A low rumble shook the deck, and an electrical hum filled the air.

Kaen's pulse quickened, knowing the TK weapon was being charged. It didn't look like anything from his vantage, but he could sense the immense power in the air. This young man in front of him had the ability to focus the very foundational energies of the universe—and Kaen had the privilege of witnessing it.

After building for nearly thirty seconds, a beam of white light shot from the *Conquest* toward its mark. At that distance, it would only take one second for the beam to strike.

Kaen watched it, heart in his throat. He braced for the impact. *This is the only way.*

The beam simply fizzled out of existence. No explosion, no vaporization… nothing. The Trol ship was unscathed.

"What happened?" he demanded.

Jason sat in stunned silence for a moment. "That's not how that was supposed to go."

"Charge was sufficient," Rianne reported. "There are traces of radiation near the target impact site but no damage."

"Was there a shield?" Jason speculated. "It should have cut through anything they had, but…" He shook his head.

Kaen didn't like the implications of the young Agent being at a loss for what the aliens could have done to deflect the weapon. By all accounts, the concentrated energy beam should have been unstoppable.

"I don't think it was a shield," Rianne replied to Jason's question. "I think the structure… absorbed the blast."

Kaen's stomach dropped. "What?"

"The radiation is now dissipating around the outer shell of the ship. I'm reviewing the readings from the moment of impact, and it's like the shell is modulating to an opposite frequency to cancel out the energy beam. That, or…" She faded out before gathering herself. "Another possibility is that it somehow diffused the blast into subspace."

"You've got to be foking kidding me," Kira muttered, slumping in her chair.

Kaen wished he could join in her reaction, but he needed to maintain decorum on behalf of the Guard. "Can you fire again? It may only have been a one-time trick."

Jason looked uncertain. "I can try."

He gripped the handholds again and concentrated. This time, he allowed the charge to build up for a full minute before releasing it.

This has to work... Kaen's chest constricted when the second beam also fizzled out.

"Looks like we can add 'death-ray-proof' to the list of ways the Trols have made life miserable for us," Kira stated under her breath.

"Torpedoes? Plasma beams? What else can you throw at it?" Kaen questioned, hearing the panic creep into his tone. *The* Conquest *was supposed to be able to take out anything. We don't* have *a more powerful weapon to bring.*

Jason laughed nervously. "Yeah, sure. I doubt they'll do anything."

A moment later, an offensive barrage fired on the alien ship. Upon impact, tiny explosive plumes erupted and were immediately extinguished.

"Damage assessment?" Kaen asked, already knowing the answer.

"Negligible," Rianne replied. "It's almost like the ship is healing itself. Would you like me to fire another round?"

Kaen exchanged glances with Kira and Jason. "We're going to need another approach."

— — —

<Well, that was anticlimactic,> Kira said to Jasmine while the colonel fumed in his chair.

<This is highly concerning.>

Kira sighed wistfully in her mind. *<You dream of firing a death-ray all your life, and then it doesn't do a bomaxed thing. That sucks any way you look at it.>*

<I'm failing to see why you're making light of this situation, Kira. The Elvar Trinary is in grave danger.>

<It's my own bizarre way of coping. It's either use humor or lose my mind from worry and fear.>

<This explains your sarcastic streak,> Jasmine observed. *<Mystery solved.>*

When Kaen made no further comment about the thwarted attack on the Trol planet-ship, Kira spoke up. "I think we need to go on board, sir. Rather, *I* need to."

Kaen scoffed. "Enough jokes, Captain. We need an actionable plan."

"I'm serious, sir," she insisted.

He looked like he was about to dismiss the statement again, then nodded. "Jason, is there somewhere the three of us could talk?"

"There's a conference room." He rose from his seat. "Rianne, withdraw and follow the Trol ship on a parallel course."

"Aye," Rianne acknowledged.

Jason directed Kira and Kaen through a doorway across the corridor from the Command Center's entrance. The room was furnished with a conference table, and the wall opposite the door had a large viewport.

Jason extended his arm for Kaen to take first pick of the seats. They settled in.

"Now, what was your crazy idea?" the colonel asked Kira.

<Great vote of confidence,> Kira thought to Jasmine.

<Can't say I blame him,> the AI shot back.

"It's not as insane as it sounds, sir," Kira began.

"I don't see how it's not." Kaen crossed his arms. "For starters, that structure is large enough that it would take days or weeks to travel any appreciable distance on foot."

For a normal person, maybe. Kira leaned forward with her elbows on her thighs. "That's assuming the destination was somewhere deep inside. I'm not suggesting I go in to plant a bomb at the center, just find an access point where I can interface with the structure to disable whatever is keeping the disruptor beam from doing its thing."

"If I may interject," Jason said, steepling his fingers, "why would you volunteer yourself for such a mission? Sounds more like a job for a team of TSS Agents."

"Kira has certain... augmentations," Kaen replied on her behalf.

"More than that, you said it yourself, Jason—you can't hear them the way I can. Are there other Agents who might have more success?" Kira asked.

"No, this doesn't seem to be a matter of raw ability level," the Agent replied. "You have a connection with these beings I don't think the TSS will be able to replicate."

Kaen folded his hands on the tabletop. "There's no argument about your being able to interface with these beings, Kira. If we're talking about disabling their defenses, then the ability to communicate hardly seems like the issue at hand."

"Isn't it, though? I'm the only person who's been able to break their telepathic hold, as far as I know."

"Regardless, they've been able to physically grab you," the colonel insisted. "I saw the first mission recording from

Gaelon—you barely made it out."

"That was before we knew about the disruptive frequency," Kira said. "That's not something they can vent into subspace or whatever. They need it to survive. It's their weakness, and we need to exploit it."

"You want to do what you did in Gaelon?" Kaen asked.

She shook her head. "No, that took everything I had and it was a fraction of this size. And there's no way we could get enough chemicals. To tackle this planet-ship, I was thinking that we need to create a temporary vulnerability—weaken it so we can use the TK weapon."

"How?" questioned Jason.

"If it's like the dwarf planet, there will be significant defenses," Kaen added. "You'd be stuck in a matter of minutes, and we'd have no way to rescue you."

"I don't have the specifics worked out, just a general concept," Kira replied.

<Oh boy, this'll be good...> Jasmine said in her mind.

"It would have to be me alone, because I'm the only one who's been able to stand up to telepathic control," Kira continued, undeterred by her AI companion. "The part about the particles being able to form bonds is a problem, but not if we can figure out a way to disrupt the frequency—maybe by charging the skin of a suit."

"Assuming that works, isn't there still an issue of how long it would take to get anywhere, once inside the ship?" Jason pointed out.

Kira looked to Kaen. "That might not be an issue."

The colonel nodded. "Perhaps it's time we fill you in on exactly what Kira can do."

CHAPTER 9

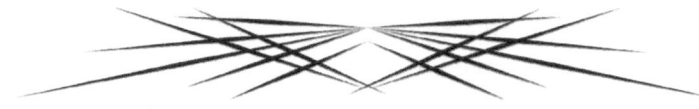

"YOU CAN CREATE localized spatial disruptions like Agents?" Jason asked with a raised eyebrow.

"That's right," Kira replied. She suspected he'd want a demonstration, but that would have to wait for later.

He hadn't been as shocked about the disclosure of her Robus state as she would have expected. Perhaps his close ties to the Priesthood's genetic experimentations had desensitized him, or maybe he was just the kind of person who took information in stride. More than anything, he'd seemed the most upset about the disclosure that a former TSS trainee had gone on to work as a twisted scientist for MTech.

"I don't understand how nanites could be responsible for those kind of abilities," the Agent continued. "And your AI, Jasmine, helps regulate the transformations?"

"That's right. Near as we can tell, the nanites maintain some sort of subspace connection to draw energy to aid in their replication, for remote communication, and to vent excess heat or whatever else they need to do," Kira explained. Leon had gone over it enough times with her that she felt reasonably confident she was using the right language. "Our science team has speculated that activating the subspace link can create a localized subspace distortion, which enables a form of super-speed—or 'stopping time', as I hear you call it in the TSS."

"It's not the explanation that's giving me pause. It's the idea that a rare genetic ability can be mimicked through nanotech. You can essentially manufacture Gifted people," Jason said.

Kaen nodded. "That appears to be what MTech was trying to do. However, the treatment didn't take in most individuals. We believe Kira's innate abilities as a Valtan telepath interacted with the nanotech—but there are only a handful of Readers on that world."

"So, it's not a work around to the Generation Cycle," Jason said to himself.

"No, we don't believe so," Kaen stated. "We'll share everything we've learned, though it appears the application of these nanites is limited."

"I know some people who'd like to make that assessment for themselves," Jason said. "But the matter at hand: what to do about this Trol vessel. I'd volunteer to go in with you, Kira, but I'm under express orders not to leave this ship."

<Orders from High Commander dad? Since when do young people listen to their parents?> Kira quipped to Jasmine.

<Not just his father. When your mom is also TSS Lead Agent and your extended family rules half of the Taran Empire, I think you're obliged to listen to their wishes.>

<That takes the fun out of things.>

"In that case," Kaen stated, "I must endorse Kira's proposal to embark on a solo mission into the Trol ship with the hope of disabling the defenses—provided a suitable countermeasure to the particle anchors can be identified."

Jason nodded. "The TSS' resources are at your disposal, if there's anything we can do to assist."

"I'll talk with my team," Kira replied. "I have an idea."

"I look forward to the details," Kaen said.

"Yes, sir. I'll get back to you soon. Thank you, Jason," Kira acknowledged.

"Of course. Here to help." He smiled.

Kira excused herself and then headed toward her temporary quarters. *<I didn't think anyone would actually go for that plan!>* she commented to Jasmine while she walked.

<You should have considered that before you volunteered,> her AI replied.

Despite her statement, Kira still believed her proposed approach had the best chance of success. If the Trols were able to dispel the force of a TK weapon capable of ripping apart a planet, then it stood to reason that they could dispatch a person with ease. She was, thus far, the only person they'd expressed long-term interest in capturing alive. That made her the singular best chance of being able to gain access to the planet-ship without being vaporized on the spot.

<Someone needed to do something,> Kira said after a pause.

<For the record, I still think your plan is madness— probably because I have to go along for the ride.>

<I won't force you to do this. If you don't think there's a chance this could work, I won't go.>

Jasmine was silent for several seconds. *<I believe that the risk to the Elvar Trinary outweighs the risk to us as individuals. Provided you can establish a sufficient safeguard against being grabbed, I agree that we should proceed.>*

<Are you sure about this, Jasmine?> Kira asked as she entered her quarters. *<Once we're committed, there's no*

turning back.>

<Kira, when Colonel Kaen and Major Sandren were interviewing me about a potential pairing with you, I told them that if I must lose my life to give others a chance, it would be a sacrifice I would gladly make. Now, faced with that reality, I stand by my word.>

Kira smiled. *<I couldn't have asked for a better partner, Jasmine.>*

<I wish we'd had the chance to get to know each other better before our pairing, but it has been a pleasure spending this past month together. All the same, I'd like to look back on this and laugh about 'that time we did a crazy thing that saved the day'.>

<We will, Jasmine.>

With her AI committed, the next step for Kira was to get the remainder of her team in place. She sent a message to Major Sandren requesting a video conference with Kyle, Nia, and Ari at the top of the hour.

When the designated time arrived, Kira settled in front of the computer terminal in her quarters. "Hi. Thank you for meeting on short notice."

"Was the explosion spectacular?" Ari asked, stars in his eyes.

Nia punched him in the shoulder. "Do you think she called us here to talk about what an awesome view it was? The plan didn't work, obviously."

Sandren cast them a stern look across the conference table. "Kira, please fill us in."

She nodded. "You're right, Nia, the plan was a bust. Turns out the Trols figured out a way to absorb the TK blast, maybe by venting it into subspace."

Everyone on the other end of the conference call leaned forward, eyes wide.

"I thought the weapon was unstoppable," Sandren

murmured.

"Needless to say, it caught us by surprise," Kira replied. "We don't know the 'how', but the blast may as well have been a flashlight shining into a black hole."

"Well, fok." Kyle crossed his arms.

"Pretty much. So, new plan," she continued. "I know you're not going to like it, but I want to go into the ship to access its central systems. I can plant a device to allow you to tap in remotely. You hack it, disable their defenses, and we blow them up. Simple."

Her team stared at her blankly.

"You do realize you've lost your mind, right?" Kyle said. "Go onto the ship... *alone*? Not a chance."

Sandren shook his head, clearly agreeing with the candid assessment.

"I've thought it through," Kira countered. She gave them an overview of her plans for a suit design to make herself untouchable.

By the end of the explanation, only Nia looked semi-convinced. "There's still any number of ways you could be captured or incapacitated. It's not worth the risk of going in alone—especially if the TSS has volunteered Agent assistance."

"Going in with a team is a bigger risk," Kira insisted. "Knowing the Trols, they'd either kill or subvert anyone else. *Me* they want. It's not worth risking other lives. I know I can beat them."

"I don't like it," Kyle maintained.

"You don't have to like it. I need you standing by to execute a remote hack. You and Nia are the best. With your skills and the TK weapon, the Trols don't stand a chance."

"There's one part you haven't covered," Sandren spoke up for the first time since the beginning of the conversation.

"What's your exit plan?"

"That will be a moving target," Kira replied.

"We never send a team in without an exit strategy," the major stated.

"We won't even know the way *in* until I find it," Kira replied. "Can't really plan a way out until we know where I'll be coming from."

He shook his head. "Unacceptable."

<He's right, Kira,> Jasmine said in her mind. *<It goes against military procedure for us to go on this mission without an egress strategy.>*

<What if it had to be one-way?>

Jasmine considered the question. *<I would still join you—but I don't think it's necessary to take that approach. There has to be a way for us to succeed and still make it out alive. We just need to figure out what the way is.>*

<Things are *pretty awesome right now. I guess it wouldn't be fair of me to break Leon's heart a second time.>*

<No, it would not.>

<All right, let's go over the schematics again and see if we can't make sense of this planet-ship.>

Kira returned her attention to the conference call. "Okay, let me get your thoughts about this beast and see what we can figure out." She shared a three-dimensional model of the Trol ship, based on what the *Conquest's* scan suite had been able to piece together, combined with the preliminary survey data.

Several details that had been missing from the long-range scan they'd viewed at Orion Station had changed their impression of the ship's operations. While the specifications about the cylinders remained unchanged, the information regarding the configuration of protrusions and the central tower-like structure had taken on significantly more detail.

What had previously looked like a solid tower, in fact, had an opening at the base. That opening had allowed the scan to get a better look inside, which had revealed a series of passageways, leading to a cavernous space, twenty-three kilometers below the tower.

"That looks a whole lot like a scaled-up version of the cavern we encountered on Gaelon," Nia observed.

"My thought, as well," Kira said. "And near as we can tell, this structure in some way functions as a hub. That means there has to be some way to interface with the ship from here."

"That's a really big assumption, Kira," Kyle said. "If you get in there and it's not like we assume, you're going to be out of luck."

"He's right," Sandren agreed. "The structure in Gaelon was likely influenced by the collaboration with the Mysaran government and MTech. There's no telling what kind of tech might be in this other thing."

"I mean, it's a foking planet-sized ship!" Ari exclaimed.

"I know it sounds crazy," Kira replied, keeping her tone calm and level, "but we have already weighed the risks. Jasmine and I agree that the threat to the Elvar Trinary is too great for me not to try this. Colonel Kaen agrees."

"I ca—"

"No," Kira cut Ari off. "This isn't up for negotiation." She paused. "Sir, may I speak freely?"

Sandren nodded. "I think you already have been. Go on."

"All of you have a home somewhere," Kira began. "You joined the Guard so you could make sure that your people would always be safe. Well, right now, my homeworld is about to be blown up by a group of aliens that doesn't even know what it's like to be an autonomous being with a body and loved ones. They're after raw minerals and a group of slaves they can possess and throw into battle with the express intent of inflicting as much suffering as possible.

"I don't know if this plan of mine will work, but there's no foking way I'm going to sit around and *hope* we come up with a solution in time to save them. My entire career in the Guard has prepared me to do whatever is necessary to protect those I love, and that's what I'm doing now. Don't try to stop me. It isn't your decision to make."

She looked at her friends' drawn faces on the viewscreen in front of her. "You don't have to like it, but I hope you'll help me. This plan has a lot better chance of success if you do your part." She focused on Sandren. "But, sir, I don't want this to be an order for anyone on the *Raven*. I want the team to be committed to this of their own accord."

After a moment of silence, Nia nodded. "You know I'll always have your back."

Kyle and Ari murmured their agreement.

"You have my support, as well," Sandren said. "I'll pilot the *Raven* myself, if I have to."

"We're just used to being the tough ones," Ari said. "Our little Kira went and got all badass on us."

She smiled. "I did, didn't I?"

"She won't be alone," Jasmine chimed in over the comm. "I'll keep her out of trouble. After all, it's my body, too, now."

"Very true," Kyle said. "I'm not sure how well we'll be able to hack this thing, but I'll give it my all."

"Thank you." Kira flashed a heartfelt smile at her team. "I wouldn't be considering this if I didn't know I had you for backup. Tell me what you'll need to make a remote connection, and we'll make the arrangements."

"They have a bunch of shielding, right?" Nia said. "You'll need to tap into a console that's wired into the ship's external communication array."

Kira frowned. "Sounds straightforward enough… if we had any idea where that was or what the components look like."

"Yeah, well, you should at least figure that much out before you go running in there with glowy eyes and claws out," Kyle responded.

"Working on it," she said. "Get yourselves to our location. I'll take care of the rest."

— — —

"I think Kira may have lost her mind," Kaen said, "but it happens to be a type of crazy I like."

Major Sandren smiled back at him over the viewscreen mounted to the wall in Kaen's temporary quarters on the *Conquest*. "I must admit, sir, I was surprised to hear you'd endorsed it."

Kaen smiled. "Kira can be very persuasive. But, truth be told, we don't have a lot of options here. We literally fired the most destructive weapon we have, and it did nothing. With no way to ramp up, we need to think smaller and more targeted. Sending in a larger team would be a surefire way to get people killed. Kira's unique abilities at least give her a shot at accomplishing the mission and getting out alive."

"She has yet to truly test the limits of her new abilities."

"Nothing like trial by fire."

"The ultimate test of autonomy."

"Indeed. If the team pulls this off, promotions are definitely in order," Kaen said. "It's long overdue."

"I heartily support an advancement. With the team operating on its own the majority of the time, rank hasn't come into play beyond the chain of command within their unit."

Kaen nodded. "They're the men and women that should be running a unit or training the next generation."

"I'd hate to break apart such a high-functioning team, but there would be a lot of value in distributing their skills," Sandren agreed.

"Then there's Kira." Kaen shook his head. "I have no idea what we should do with her."

"The present team dynamic no longer reflects the best use of her skills. However, planning out a future path for her is a discussion I think she should be a part of—after we've dealt with the Trols."

"Without a doubt," Kaen agreed. "She has great things ahead of her."

Sandren nodded. "I'll be honored to look back and say I was here for this event."

"This upcoming encounter will surely be one for the history books."

"A daring plan. If anyone can pull it off, it's Kira and the rest of her team," the major agreed. "But, all the same, what are our contingencies if it doesn't work?"

"I'm working with the TSS to put backup precautions in place," Kaen told him. "Planetary shields. The generators likely couldn't withstand a long-term assault, but it might buy some extra time. And, if nothing else, they will offer peace of mind to the civilian population."

Sandren nodded. "One can never underestimate the value of psychological well-being. Maintaining order on the affected worlds will be critical."

"It will, but that's not your concern. I'll make the necessary preparations in the Elvar Trinary while you're in transit."

"Yes, sir."

"There is one thing I need your help coordinating," Kaen said. "We'll require a way to interface with the ship in the event our normal wireless or hardwire connectivity methods don't work. There's a specialist on Leon's team who works with bioelectric interfaces, yes?"

"I believe so."

"Get the team on the issue. I want a fallback strategy ready, if it's needed."

"Consider it done, sir," Sandren acknowledged.

"Thank you, see you soon. We'll have everything else ready for the team when you arrive."

CHAPTER 10

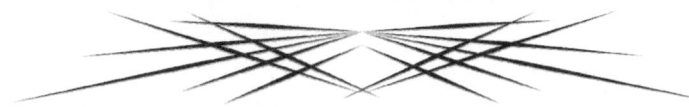

UN-FOKING-BELIEVABLE. Ellen raced into the open area at the center of the government office that had been functioning as her administrative headquarters, dubbed 'Ops Central'. The nickname was a little overkill, but everyone in the office knew what it meant.

The sun had yet to rise for the day, but she'd already been awake for hours. Since receiving the alert from Joris about the impending attack, she'd been coordinating with Guard and TSS representatives about receiving delivery of defensive tech to augment Mysar's standard planetary shield, which deflected minor space debris.

The rest of her team had yet to arrive. Her message in the wee hours of the morning had no doubt alarmed them, but she'd kept the reason for the early meeting to herself for the time being. Some news was better delivered in person.

Ellen powered up the conference table while she waited and loaded in the schematics for the new planetary shield components.

While she queued up the final pieces of her forthcoming presentation, Fiona wandered in. Despite the early hour, she still had her trademark polished appearance.

"Ellen, what's going on?" she asked.

"I'll go crazy if I need to repeat myself for every person who walks through the door. Have a seat—I'll explain soon."

Fiona cracked a smile, though her face was lined with worry. "I guess that was the wrong question. A better one may be, 'how bad is it?' "

Ellen cast her a level gaze across the conference table in response.

"I guess the fact that you called us here for an 04:30 meeting says it all." Fiona slumped into a chair without her usual poise.

Trisha was the next to arrive, at almost the same time as Edgar and Marcy, who'd both been serving as managers on various special projects to restore the government. The remaining half-dozen staffers trickled in over the next three minutes.

When the ten attendees were seated, Ellen stood up at the head of the table.

"Thank you for coming in so early. I asked each of you here because I know you can be trusted. You each played a part in the Trol eradication last month, so I don't need to fill you in or impress upon you how dangerous they are."

With that, everyone's faces paled. A few people swore under their breath.

Fiona sat, calmly as ever, with her hands folded in her lap. "Did you find more of them?"

"Not exactly," Ellen replied. "More, they found us." She brought up an image of the Trol ship, which Kaen had relayed from the Guard's ocana.

The ship appeared as a meter-wide sphere hovering above the center of the conference table. At that size, the dish suspected of being a weapon looked like little more than a child's toy.

"Is that a planet?" Trisha asked, tilting her head.

"No, looks like a probe," Edgar replied. "See those mechanical components?"

"You're both right, in a way," Ellen cut in. "This graphic doesn't give a good sense of scale. In reality, this thing here is the same size as Mysar."

Trisha's jaw dropped. "No *way*."

The frown Fiona had been sporting since the image appeared deepened. "So, this is why we were called here. Is it the Trols? Is this coming our way?"

Ellen nodded grimly. "I won't pretend to make this anything other than what it is. There's a planet-sized ship headed for this system, and we believe the intent is to harvest the natural resources of these worlds."

Gasps sounded around the table.

"What does that mean, 'harvest'?" Trisha asked.

"Everything is speculation," Ellen said. "All we know for sure is that the object is on a direct course for this system, and it's the Trols. Based on what we've seen them do already, it's not a leap to say this ship is capable of much, much worse."

The attendees all started asking questions at once, and Ellen held up her hands. "I know you want answers, but talking over each other or panicking won't help us prepare. Let me finish reviewing the plan, and then you can clarify your responsibilities to help see us through this crisis."

They returned their attention to her, but most still squirmed in their seats.

"The Empire is sending augmentations of our existing

planetary shields," she continued. "While Mysar isn't officially in the Empire, it's fair to say that we've been courting each other for the past month. Since Elusia *is* a member world and is facing the same threat, the decision was made to outfit the three worlds in our system with the same technology, as to not leave one a more enticing target than the others. We need to be unified to get through this.

"However, these shields are only a precaution. The Guard and TSS are presently launching a joint strategic assault on the Trol ship. I don't know the details, so don't bother asking, but I've been assured that there's a high chance of success. Assuming it *is* successful, the ship won't get anywhere close to us.

"Getting the Empire's shield tech installed is going to take all of us working smart. We have a lot to do to get the pieces in place. A handful of the Guard's tech specialists will be here to oversee the installation, but they aren't enough to get it done. You'll each have assignments for gathering the resources and coordinating the necessary pieces. Trisha and I will oversee the operation from here."

Ellen advanced the presentation. The holographic image changed to a schematic of a field generator. Nine such devices were positioned at equidistant points around the planet.

"Each of the rest of you will be responsible for overseeing the installation of the upgrades at one of the sites, serving as a liaison with the Guard on behalf of the Mysaran government. This is the critical part: only you and the Guard tech will know what these upgrades are for. We don't have time to conduct a proper briefing for the maintenance workers at the outposts, and dropping the news like this would result in widespread panic. Your job is to go there and act like everything is routine."

Fiona raised her hand slightly, and Ellen gave her a nod of consent. "Won't it be pretty obvious that this isn't routine, what with the Tararian Guard showing up to help and the fast timeline?"

"A good-faith gift from the Empire, on behalf of Elusia's recent reunification," Ellen replied. "Or, that's what's we'll tell them, if asked. The Guard was coming to install Elusia's standard shield upgrade, as part of the arrangement, and they're on a tight timeline to complete it before moving on to other projects. For all anyone on Mysar knows, the Empire always moves this quickly."

"And what *is* the timeline?" Fiona asked.

"Right." Ellen took a deep breath. "We have three days before the ship arrives in the system. The Guard transports with the shield components will be here this afternoon, giving you time to travel to the generators and build some rapport with the workers."

"Half a day won't get us much bonding," Edgar said.

Ellen shrugged. "Bring some cookies. A few hours is better than nothing."

She made rapid entries on the touch-surface tabletop. Briefs popped up in front of each of the attendees.

"There are your post assignments," she continued. "I know some of those are the kind of locations you'd never want to visit in your life, but thank you in advance for taking one for the team."

Edgar looked up at her, his eyes wide with concern. "The equator?"

"Yeah, I know. A little toasty down there. But the shuttles will dock inside, you'll be fine." She cast her gaze around the table. "The assignments include your transportation details. Review the file. Come find me if you have questions, but it's better if you figure out an answer for yourself. You'll be in charge on the site, so get used to it. Dismissed."

She leaned against the side wall of the conference room while everyone departed.

Only Fiona stayed back. "Keeping Trisha here? Why not me?" she asked when they were alone. Her tone wasn't angry, more surprised.

"I would love to have you here, Fi, but the generator outside the capital is the control station for the entire network. I don't want to worry about it getting messed up."

Fiona crossed her arms and narrowed her eyes slightly. "There's more to it than that."

"This really isn't the time to discuss it," Ellen said, pushing off the wall.

The other woman blocked her path. "This is about the government leadership, isn't it?"

Ellen checked that no one was close enough to listen in. She sighed. "Okay, yes, there is a political component to this. I talked with Joris, and he'd like to make a play for a presidency over the three worlds, with a governor on each. I think Mysar needs a local face. Since you've made it clear you don't want the top spot, I think Trisha is the best choice."

"So, you want her here at the center of operations, to see if she can handle it, and if she can, to get others used to seeing her in that role."

"Yeah, pretty much."

"Does she know you're doing that?"

Ellen shrugged. "If she does, she hasn't indicated as much. I've never seen her express interest in having a bigger leadership role, but she's also never dismissed it as directly as you have. What better trial run than a crisis?"

"She did keep her cool with the Trol situation last time

around, and she knows the operations inside and out."

"Her résumé is a little light on authoritative positions, but at this point, that doesn't matter. She's smart and committed—the rest can come with time and experience."

Fiona nodded. "I'd vote for her."

Ellen smiled. "Well, if she can win *you* over, then she's a shoo-in."

"All right. I guess we should probably save the world, then, so she actually has a planet left to govern."

"Not a bad idea."

Fiona took a deep breath. "Okay, I'll get to it. See you on the other side."

"Good luck. We'll be in touch."

Ellen cleared any evidence of the meeting's content from the conference room, then she headed to her office. After verifying that everyone was clear on their assignments, she set about making the final logistical arrangements for the arrival of the Guard shield equipment.

An hour later, when the sun was finally beginning to peek over the horizon, Ellen's desktop chirped with an incoming communication from Elusia.

"President Joris, I didn't expect to hear from you again today," she greeted.

"I wanted to make sure that everything was on track," he replied. "Did you get everything you need from Colonel Kaen?"

"Yes, the installation project is underway," Ellen said. "They took the news better than I feared they might."

"You showed them?"

"It didn't seem right to hide the details. What better way to impress the importance of their actions than to show what we're up against?"

He nodded. "I agree. Mitchell Korwen, on the other hand, seems like he'd be better suited to living under a rock."

"Uh oh." Ellen's brows drew together. "What happened?"

"Well, I reached out to him earlier, right after I spoke with you. It was the middle of the afternoon local time on Valta, so he was in his office. I expected it to be a civil call from one leader to another, but he laughed when I told him."

"That doesn't sound very mayoral."

"To say the least." Joris sighed. "I emphasized that the situation wasn't going to go away on its own, but he still seems… reluctant to take it seriously."

Ellen rubbed her eyes. "I didn't think it would be a problem. He always seemed so level-headed while I was growing up."

"Age can do strange things to people."

"Or maybe he was never the leader I remember him being as a kid."

She had fond memories of her youth, and, admittedly, there was never much conflict on Valta. The biggest issue they'd ever faced in Tribeca was having too many traveler visa applications during the peak summer festival season. Someone in Mayor Korwen's position needed to be a friendly face for the travel brochures—not a person responsible for addressing extreme safety concerns related to planetary affairs. Perhaps his years of such low-stakes governing had made him blind to a genuine crisis.

"Where do things with Valta stand now?" she asked.

"The Guard will be arriving with its shipment in three hours. At this point, I'm not positive he'll offer any local assistance. If he doesn't, the number of conversations we'll need to have to get that equipment installed in time would delay us—to the point that I don't know if we could complete the install before the Trol ship is due to arrive."

Ellen swore under her breath. "Do you want me to talk with him? I don't know if it would make a difference, but maybe hearing from a local would help."

"At this point, I will happily explore any option. Please, do what you can."

She nodded. "All right. I'll get back to you soon."

Ugh, Mayor Korwen... why are you being difficult? She wiped her hands down her face.

She had no idea how best to approach him. He had always been a fixture in the small Tribeca community, managing duties related to the town's ecotourism more than any real civic issues. She wasn't sure if years of dealing with such minimal concerns had made him soft, or if he was just in denial about the danger his world now faced, but she couldn't allow Valta to be in harm's way. If she had to go to her homeworld herself to make sure it was protected, she'd hop on the first available ship.

Having never spoken with the mayor directly, Ellen contacted the reception desk at Tribeca City Hall and requested a transfer.

"Who shall I tell him is calling?" the receptionist asked. "This line is marked as Gilbert Jern. You don't sound much like a Gilbert."

"No, I'm using his office. My name is Ellen Calleti," she replied. "I'm the press secretary for President Joris of Elusia."

"This is a Mysaran access code."

"It's complicated. Please, I need to speak with Mayor Korwen right away."

The receptionist took a slow breath. "One moment."

The line went quiet for five seconds, followed by a beep as the video call connected on her monitor.

"Hello?" an older man answered. His white, bushy

eyebrows were even wilder than Ellen remembered.

"Mister Mayor, my name is Ellen Calleti. I grew up in Tribeca."

The mayor placed a pensive hand on his chin. "Philip and Martha's daughter?"

"Yes, that's right."

"Ah." He nodded. "There aren't many violet-eyed children. I remember you and your brother."

"That's us." She smiled. "Well, I'm working with President Joris now on Elusia, though I'm currently on assignment on Mysar. I understand that the president has already reached out to you regarding a security threat to our system."

"Ah, yes." The mayor scoffed. "And you thought if I heard from a local, I might listen closer to what was being said?"

"Forgive my frankness, sir, but this isn't a matter of opinion. An alien ship the size of Mysar is three days from entering the Elvar Trinary. If it arrives, and augmented shields aren't active on Valta, the planet is at extreme risk of destruction. All you need to do is authorize the installation of the equipment upgrades at the generator outposts."

"There are two key facts you're not taking into account, young lady."

Ellen resisted rolling her eyes. *Oh, this will be good.*

"First, I'm the mayor of Tribeca—I don't speak for the whole planet." He leaned forward toward the camera integrated in his monitor. "Moreover, Valta isn't an Empire world. Are we to trust that this equipment installation doesn't come with strings attached?"

"Membership status in the Taran Empire has nothing to do with this. Why would you turn down protection from a threat?"

"All I see is a holographic image. For all I know, this is a ploy to give the Empire a backdoor into taking over Valta to exploit its unique properties. There might not *be* an alien ship at all!"

Ellen stared at him with disbelief. "You think the Guard would mislead you like that?"

"I know nothing of the central Taran worlds other than they deal in wars and try to sway others to their will. Valta is a small, peaceful world. We need no part in such things."

"I can appreciate your position, Mister Mayor, but time necessitates that I be blunt: if the Empire wished to take over Valta, they would simply take it. *Allowing* them to install equipment doesn't change anything, other than protect the planet from the *real* threat."

"I don't appreciate your tone."

"Well, I don't appreciate you refusing to participate in this project." Ellen glared at him. "I recommended President Joris reach out to you because I thought you would be able to help. I see that I was sorely mistaken."

"I know you grew up here, and your parents have always been upstanding members of this community, but you left home long ago, Ellen. You are now a citizen of Elusia, and I have no innate trust in you."

This was a mistake. Ellen took a deep breath. "I only want what's best for Valta."

The old man shook his head. "You have other worlds to worry about now."

"The Elvar Trinary will be united, whether you go along with this plan or not. The certainty, however, is that if you don't cooperate, we will come by force, and you'll have no say in the future dealings of the world."

He scoffed. "You have no authority."

If power is what motivates him, then I need to hit him where it hurts. Ellen curled her lips, eyes narrow. "Not on my own. But, unlike you, I have made friends with very powerful people. They care about the system's well-being, too. That equipment is getting installed, no matter what you do now. Whether or not you have a political future in Tribeca, however, is still up for discussion." Ellen folded her hands on the desktop. "So, I'll ask you again. Will you facilitate the Guard's access to the shield generation stations?"

The mayor sat up straighter in his chair. "When you put it like that, perhaps this is the time to start a relationship with the Empire on the right foot."

"I'm so glad to hear you've reconsidered. The Guard techs will be in touch when they arrive. Select nine staff to serve as liaisons with the maintenance team at the stations—keep the reason for the installation need-to-know."

The mayor nodded. "Fine. But if the Empire wrongs us, you'll need to live with the fact that you did this to your home."

"I'll know I *saved* my home. I can live with that just fine."

CHAPTER 11

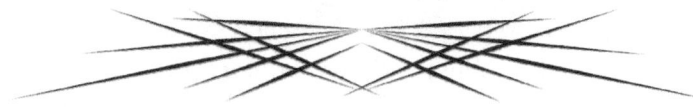

LEON HAD TOLD himself he'd get used to Kira going off on missions, but that was easier said than done. As the hours passed without hearing from her, he found himself growing increasingly concerned that something was wrong.

This should have been a quick op—get there, blow the ship up, come home. Why the delay? He didn't have an explanation.

Even Jack and Tess were quieter than usual. As much as he tried to dismiss his worry, it kept nagging at him.

"Should we have heard something by now?" he asked them as the afternoon turned to evening.

Tess turned around from her station. "I don't want to feed any concerns you may have, but yeah, I kinda did expect there to be something on the local Net by now."

"Blowing up a massive planet-ship is a pretty big deal," Jack agreed. "Footage of that would be circulated as soon as it was available."

"Unless they opted to keep it covert, so no one got freaked out about there maybe being other alien ships out there," Leon replied.

The two lab techs exchanged glances. "Yeah, no," Jack said.

Even Leon didn't buy his own rationale.

"Just because they haven't fired on the ship yet doesn't mean anything is wrong," Tess added. "And regardless, I'm sure Kira is fine."

"Yeah, I know." He slumped in his seat.

"Assignments like this are always the worst," Tess said. "I dated a soldier on one of the special ops teams for a while. I eventually got used to him going off on routine missions— protection detail, retrieval, what have you. But every so often, he'd go out and wouldn't tell me anything about the mission. Whenever he said he was heading out but got really quiet after he told me, I'd know it was one of those… the sort that sometimes not every member of the team would come back from. I hated every second he was gone."

Jack raised an eyebrow. "When was this? You never mentioned him before."

"We were only together for about five months, and it was before you and I met. I guess it never came up."

Not sure if that was meant to be helpful, but it wasn't. Leon turned back to his workstation. "Like you said, I'm sure she's fine."

"Sorry, I—"

Tess cut off when the door suddenly opened.

Major Sandren popped his head inside. "Good, you're all here. I need you to do something for me."

Leon came to attention. "Of course, sir."

The major stepped inside and closed the door behind him. "What I'm about to tell you doesn't leave this room."

The three scientists nodded.

"The TK weapon had no effect on the enemy ship,"

Sandren revealed.

"Stars! Really?" Jack exclaimed.

"Obviously, we don't want word of that getting around. We have a new plan, which involves going aboard the alien ship to form a direct interface. If we can temporarily disable the countermeasures, we can use the *Conquest*'s TK weapon and end this."

Leon's stomach dropped. "*Who's* going aboard?"

"Kira volunteered." Sandren held up his hand. "And before you say anything, I objected, too. She made a clear case for why she's the only person equipped to go, and I begrudgingly have to agree."

Even without being a part of that conversation, Leon knew exactly what reasons she would have cited. And it did make sense… He hated that.

"What's this favor you need?" Leon asked, trying to focus on the things that were within his control.

"I need you to go over the scans from the ship—I'll get you access to the latest data collected on the *Conquest*. Our plan hinges on being able to interface with the alien ship so Kyle and Nia can hack it, but it's unclear if we'll be able to make a standard connection, either physical or wireless," Sandren explained. "I'd like you to apply what you've learned about the structures in Gaelon to see if you can devise a backup method of interfacing with the Trols' systems."

Tess looked at Leon across the lab. "We could use the Gaelon debris."

He nodded. "Yeah, and look at the logs from the Orion Station hack to isolate the signal that activated it."

"I should be able to establish a datalink protocol based on that info," Jack said.

Sandren smiled. "Sounds like you have it handled. We'll

need your solution in twelve hours."

Leon sighed. *Of* course *they do.*

But it was for Kira, so they had to make it happen.

— — —

With her team in transit, all Kira could do was wait for their arrival. However, sitting around idly wasn't her style.

She rolled onto her back on the bunk in her temporary quarters. She had the room to herself, but it was less than three meters wide and four deep. If she spent another minute cooped up, she was going to lose it.

<Ugh, there has to be some sort of gym on this behemoth of a ship, right?> she asked Jasmine.

<Yes. Two decks down and aft. I was about to suggest we go.>

<Feeling a little antsy yourself?>

<Actually, my reasoning was that this is our only opportunity to practice intentional transformations before we enter the Trol ship,> the AI replied.

<Ah, that's a good point.>

Kira hadn't considered that part of the plan. With an electrostatic skin in place over her armor, the Trol particles would theoretically be unable to latch onto her and secure her to the ground like they'd done on Gaelon. She'd been so focused on that physical element that she'd been neglecting the telepathic part.

When presenting the idea, she had brought forth the pertinent fact that she could resist succumbing to telepathic influence, unlike others. However, she'd forgotten *why.*

It wasn't a unique resistance thanks to her own telepathic skills or a natural ability. Rather, it was a byproduct of shifting to and from her Robus state. Though neither her innate abilities or the new nanites were a sufficient safeguard alone, the combination of attributes had proven effective in breaking the Trols' telepathic bonds, and Jasmine's presence ensured that she would always be able to transform when she needed to.

Even with that winning combination, though, there were still risks. Kira had only transformed completely a handful of times before—mostly due to a lack of adequate practice space at Guard headquarters and on the *Raven*—so Jasmine didn't yet have sufficient data to regulate her physiology to its optimal performance. The only way to gather that data was to go through the exercise.

<*Tell me where to go,*> Kira said to the AI. <*We'll kick everyone out of the gym and see what we can do together.*>

<*I suggest an empty cargo bay instead. It's a much larger space,*> Jasmine countered.

<*Lead the way.*>

Jasmine directed Kira toward an empty cargo bay in the bowels of the ship. The vessel was enormous compared to the *Raven*—or most other ships she'd been on. Despite its size, it managed to maintain the feeling of a place where people could live for an extended amount of time. Subtle decorations on the walls and furnishings in the common areas lent a communal atmosphere, which was evident in informal gatherings between groups of soldiers.

Several individuals cast her an evaluating look as she passed through the halls, and a few nodded in greeting. She smiled and nodded back, but none of the exchanges lasted for more than a second.

<*Do they know who I am?*> she asked Jasmine.

<*Some might, but don't let it go to your head. I suspect most*

of those looks are because you're dressed as a Guard officer.>

<Oh yeah, good point.>

<I did promise that I'd have a lot of those.>

Kira chuckled in her mind. *<And you have followed through.>*

The corridor leading to the cargo bay access door was empty, aside from two workers making plans for after their shifts ended.

<Should we be planning our own victory party?> Kira asked Jasmine.

<Might be getting a little ahead of ourselves,> the AI replied in her mind.

<I'm telling you, knowing that there's a cake waiting for us would be extra motivation to succeed.>

Jasmine sighed. *<If that's what gets you fired up, go for it. I think you already have another, more compelling, reason to complete this mission.>*

Kira smiled to herself. *She's right. Leon is waiting for me.* As much as she loved cake, Leon would win out every time.

Upon reaching the target cargo bay, Jasmine got a lock override for the door from the ship's AI—one of the CACI clones.

The entry led to a balcony overlooking the open space standing three decks tall, seventy meters wide, and a hundred deep. Along the back wall, a massive hatch provided direct access for loading in cargo. Completely empty at the moment, it would provide unobstructed training ground to hone her transformation skills.

She descended the side stairway one story to the deck. *<Ready to give it a go?>*

<Yes. Let's start with a simple shift.>

Kira took a deep breath and centered her mind. Her

previous shifting attempts had been made while she was in an agitated state, specifically at times when she was angry. Such potent emotions clouded judgment, though, and she needed to learn to transform without losing her cool.

Jasmine began altering the chemical mixture in her body and brain to mimic the state that had triggered past transformations. With the physiological change, Kira had the sudden urge to punch something, but she kept the impulse in check.

I'm in control. I dictate what I do with these powers.

Tingling spread from her fingertips and forehead toward her core. She looked down at her hands and saw metallic scales spreading across her arms under her shipsuit's sleeves, and her silvery nails were extending into razor-sharp claws.

<I don't feel any pain,> she commented to Jasmine.

<I'm blocking it in your brain.>

<Thanks.>

Kira flexed her arms and legs when the transformation was complete, her shipsuit taut around her broadened shoulders. While still not as strapped as the soldiers on her team, she stood at least six centimeters taller than normal, and the nanite augmentations made her limbs appear thicker and more toned. She ran her tongue along the back side of the nanite fangs.

Even her senses were enhanced—noticing the metallic scent of the filtered air, minute scuffs on the deck tiles from where a crate had been dragged, or even the faint echoes of the conversation in the hall that had previously been undetectable.

The amount of sensory input at her disposal threatened to overwhelm her, so she did her best to block it out and focus on her own physical state.

<All right, let's see what I can do.>

As a baseline, she began by jumping straight into the air.

The first attempt was a little under two meters, close to her standing height.

<Based on the configuration of nanite enhancements within your musculoskeletal system, I believe you'll see the best results with a running start toward a leap,> Jasmine recommended.

Kira ran halfway across the depth of the bay, then turned back to face the elevated entry platform. <I apologize in advance if this fails miserably.>

<It's the only way we'll learn! Go for it.>

She took off at a brisk jog, careful to hold herself back from going into super-speed mode. Ten meters from the platform, she bumped up the pace a notch and then leaped for the platform.

The air whooshed past her as she extended her clawed hands for the railing. It was so close—almost within her grasp. Her claws grazed the bottom lip of the platform.

<Oops.>

She plummeted downward.

The deck met her face and chest, knocking the air from her lungs. "Ow," she moaned, rolling to her side.

<Why didn't you land on your feet?> Jasmine chastised.

<Lost my bearings, I guess. I was so sure I was going to make it.>

<You dialed back a little too much.>

Kira rose to her feet and gingerly rubbed her sternum, careful to keep her claws angled away from her body. <Yeah, I got that.>

<You're not hurt. Let's go again.>

For the second attempt, Kira took a faster pace and also waited an extra stride before pushing off the deck. This time, she sailed through the air and was able to easily grasp the upper rung of the railing.

<Good. Again.>

Jasmine had her complete the exercise another five times at various speeds and leap points to establish the variables.

<Now, try leaping over the top of the railing,> she instructed.

The first two attempts resulted in Kira's face becoming acquainted with the deck of the entry platform, her foot having caught while trying to clear the rail.

"Oof." Kira picked herself off the deck. "I didn't think this exercise was going to beat me up."

<Your med-nano will have you healed in less than an hour, quit complaining.>

Kira rolled her eyes. *<Are you sure you weren't a drill sergeant in a past life?>*

<Quite sure, but it does sound like it would be fun to push bodies and minds to their limits,> Jasmine replied.

<'Biomedical specialist AI' just moved to the top of my list of drill sergeant types you don't ever want to get, for what it's worth.

<Oh, this isn't boot camp, Kira. You get me all the time, and I'm in your mind so I know exactly how much you can take. Now, jump off this balcony!>

With a heavy sigh, Kira complied.

<Sprints, far wall and back.>

She dashed across the room, closing the hundred meters in a second.

Truth be told, she didn't mind being put through her paces. It was exhilarating to finally be able to let loose outside the context of facing down an enemy, to practice in a place where failure didn't mean death for herself or her teammates.

Kira hadn't had such a free session in years. She regularly trained with her team, sure, but she'd always had something to prove to them, with her smaller stature. With them, she'd never wanted to misstep, so she always played it safe.

Alone in a room with Jasmine, however, she could fall on her face repeatedly and no one would know.

<*Good. Quick rest, and then we'll go again,*> Jasmine told her.

Kira stopped to stretch.

"Fascinating," a voice said from above, startling her.

She spun around to see Jason Sietinen looking over the railing. "Stars! When did you get here?" she exclaimed.

"A minute ago, maybe. I wasn't sure what to make of your statements earlier when you talked about the Robus state. Have to say, this isn't quite what I envisioned."

Right, that. Kira reverted to her normal appearance. "I wasn't expecting anyone to look in on this session." At least he hadn't shown up while she was a crumpled heap on the deck.

"You didn't think you'd be able to get by without a firsthand demonstration of your abilities, did you?" He jogged down the steps to the lower deck.

"Hadn't occurred to me, honestly."

The young Agent approached her. "A genuine alien hybrid… The scales are bonded nanites?"

"Yes, as near as we can tell."

"How strange. The Aesir have never mentioned tech like this." He looked her over, seemingly searching for where the nanites had disappeared to.

"Sorry, what?"

He shook his head. "Never mind. I'm sure you've already been studied more than you like."

"The Guard's science team pretty much just calls me 'Weirdo' now." She was joking, but it wasn't far from the truth.

"Being unique isn't a bad thing. Challenging and isolating,

sometimes, but not bad." It was clear from Jason's tone that he was speaking from personal experience.

<Imagine having his lineage—the expectations of power and responsibility,> Jasmine commented.

<No wonder he wants to be on a first-name basis. How else do you try to connect?> Kira smiled at him. "It's all about finding your place in a community, right?"

"Very much so. And you've found that in the Guard?"

"They were my family well before this transformation."

He nodded. "Well, if you ever need other outlets, know there's an open door to the TSS."

"Thank you, I appreciate that."

"In the meantime," he began circling her, "I'd like to see how you can move with these new augmentations. Maybe a little sparring?"

<Actually, it would be helpful for you to practice shifting into the Robus state while in combat,> Jasmine said. *<I have most of the other data I need to guide your state while we're in the ship.>*

Kira tilted her head as she looked Jason over. "What would it do for my career prospects to land a few blows on a senior TSS Agent?"

He smiled back. "You sound awfully confident you'll be able to hit me."

She smirked. "You saw that blur running across the floor. Still want to extend the offer?"

"What kind of an Agent would I be if I shied away from a challenge? Bring it on."

Kira assumed a combat pose. "All right, but don't say I didn't warn you." With Jasmine's help, she initiated a transformation into the Robus state.

The Agent took a step back as her claws and fangs formed.

"Wow, that's really something."

Kira lunged for him, aiming her claws for clothing rather than bare flesh. The world appeared to slow down around her as she moved at the end of a self-generated spatial distortion.

Centimeters before she was about to make contact, Jason calmly stepped to the side to avoid her attack.

"The fok?" Kira's time perception returned to normal.

"You can't rely on speed alone when you're dealing with opponents who share your skills," Jason said. "The Trols have created others with enhance speed, correct?"

Kira's brow knitted. "Yeah…"

"Then it is best to assume you may face them. Be prepared to fight on their level, or you will be at a disadvantage."

"What would I do differently?"

Jason grinned. "That's what I'm here to show you."

CHAPTER 12

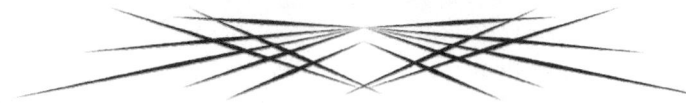

THE ENSUING LESSON was more illuminating than Kira could have ever anticipated. Her previous approach had been to jump into super-speed and remain in that state for as long as possible. Through Jason's instruction, she learned strategies to employ bursts of speed to manipulate the enemy—minimizing her energy expenditure while inflicting maximum damage.

After half an hour of practice, she did manage to land a few blows on the Agent—even though he was probably going easy on her. All the same, she felt much more prepared to face any Trol combatants she may encounter on the alien ship.

"I really appreciate the pointers," she said.

Jason rubbed his side, where Kira had landed her last kick. "Happy to help. I want to give you your best chance of success."

Kira leaned against the bulkhead to rest. "It's still crazy for me to think that *I'm* going up against these guys, instead of someone like... well, *you*."

"Don't denigrate your abilities, Kira. I *wasn't* going easy on you, despite what you may think. You can hold your own in hand-to-hand combat."

She smirked. "I wasn't trying to show off or anything."

"Sure." He flashed a playful smile back.

"I'm just happy I can keep up with you on *some* level. You Agents can do all sorts of fancy things."

"You shouldn't take my abilities as a representation of an average Agent."

Kira waved her hand. "Well, yeah, using the *Conquest*'s TK weapon requires a lot of raw power. But can't most of you, like, astral project and teleport and stuff?"

Jason laughed. "Is that what they say about TSS Agents?"

"I mean, I've heard…"

He kept chuckling. "Yeah, no. First of all, the closest thing we have to teleporting is a TSD Arch, but that's essentially a portal through subspace between two proximate devices. 'Stopping time'—as we've demonstrated in this practice session—isn't teleporting at all. As for astral projection, well… yes, a few people can do it, but it's far less common than even the ability to create localized spatial disruptions."

"Then how did that get to be such a common misconception?" Kira wondered aloud.

"I suspect there were stories from the Bakzen War. The Priesthood was big on spreading misinformation—particularly anything that painted Gifted as being untrustworthy outsiders. Former TSS trainees like Monica Waylon certainly haven't helped that perception." His face darkened.

"I'm getting the impression you looked her up?"

Jason nodded. "My dad actually had a vague recollection of her—not many trainees leave after the first year, especially from the Primus class. Turns out that she was in the cohort after his."

"Small universe."

"More than you know." He shook his head. "At any rate, while she had very promising test scores, there were some... disciplinary issues. If she hadn't elected to drop out of the training program, it's possible she would have been reassigned based on moral and ethical grounds."

Kira's eyes widened. "That happens?"

"Extremely rarely. There are extensive psych evals before someone is admitted. I mean, we're pretty much training people to be living weapons. You don't want to grant that kind of power to a psychopath."

"Yeah, but she still seemed to learn plenty of skills all the same."

"That was one of the reasons I wanted to look her up. She actually came from Valdos III, which is a conservative world, but one of the only places that permitted the open practice of telekinesis while the Priesthood was still in power. I suspect that background is what enabled her to learn advanced skills without training through the TSS."

"I wonder what made her go down such a dark path?" Kira mused.

Jason shrugged. "A thirst for power can all too often lead to blind ambition. Once you make one ethical compromise, it's a slippery slope."

"I've always thought about telepathy that way, too. You need to be careful what kind of precedent you set."

"We have a clear code of conduct for that very reason."

Kira studied him. "All right, so tell me... behind the ethics and codes, what's the truth about Agents and what you can do?"

He smiled. "For the most part, we're normal people. Our abilities are just a part of who we are, and we strive to use that power to help others. Telepathy is the most basic skill, then small object levitation, manipulating electromagnetic fields and the like." He conjured an energy orb in the palm of his hand, a casual action in a split second.

Kira jumped back. "Whoa!"

<*That would have changed the outcome of your sparring,*> Jasmine commented.

<*I'll say!*> Kira stared at the energy orb with open awe. <*Why, again, isn't this guy taking on the Trols instead?*>

<*Because sometimes finesse is more effective than raw power, and no one is more committed to successfully completing this mission than you.*>

<*Too bad I can't also conjure energy orbs.*>

<*We'll make up for it in other ways.*>

"This kind of thing," Jason went on while he tossed the orb between his hands, "looks fancier than it is. Our ability to manipulate energy fields allows us to concentrate ambient forces into manifestations like this." He dissipated the orb. "The *Conquest*'s weapon is a scaled-up version of that. Most people can focus a concentrated energy field the size of their fist, but very few can withstand channeling the energy needed to do large-scale damage."

"And, yet, you're here to operate the TK weapon alone," Kira stated. Suddenly, she had a new appreciation for the extent of young man's abilities.

He shook his head. "The Trol ship, despite its size, doesn't have the dense mass of a planet. A few TK blasts should have been enough to break it apart."

She only stared at him in response.

"Okay, admittedly, that's a bigger feat than I'm giving it credit for."

Kira raised an eyebrow. "You think?"

"Anyway, we weren't anticipating the initial attack to be

completely ineffective. It goes to show that all power is relative."

"My fear is that we haven't seen the limits of the Trols' tech yet," Kira murmured.

"From what you've said, it's not the tech that concerns me. Their resistance to the attack may be a matter of the beings' unique properties—the subspace connection on a nanoscopic level. Subspace's properties are so different from physical reality that it requires an alternate offensive approach."

"Can you fight them, if I don't succeed?" Kira asked.

He hesitated. "We'll always find a way to protect our fellow Tarans."

"I sense a 'but'," she prompted.

"Honestly, I've never faced an enemy like this before. *You* have. I'm confident the combined forces of the Guard and TSS could stop them in the end, but whether that solution came in time to save your home system… there's no guarantee."

She took a deep breath. "Then it falls to me. I'll come through."

He nodded. "I have no doubt you will."

— — —

Kaen disconnected from the remote video feed to the cargo room and leaned back in the desk chair. He wished he'd been able to test Kira himself, but he was the first to admit she had speed and strength on her side. Jason had made for a much more suitable opponent.

Being a third-party observer had also afforded Kaen the chance to objectively assess Kira's state of mind—how she was handling the stress of having an entire mission hinging on her. She had given him no cause for concern; if anything, she seemed to be in good spirits.

Considering that the future of an entire system is presently in her hands, that's a win for all of us. Even though it bolstered his confidence that the mission would be successful, he couldn't neglect the contingency plans.

Beyond the danger to the Elvar Trinary, the Guard was at risk. The Trols had broken in once, and though they'd been blocked from reentering the system for now, the aliens could potentially get an infusion of new resources from the Elvar Trinary, which could bolster their strength. As sickening as it was to think about that potential, Kaen needed to make sure the Guard finished getting its own augmented defenses in place.

He established a secure comm link to Orion Station and initiated a video call with Major Olvera.

The chief of security picked up. "Sir, what can I do for you?"

"How much have you heard about my mission on the *Conquest*?"

"I know it's connected to the Trols and the attack on the base, but not much beyond that."

"Well, it's time I explained," he replied.

She nodded her understanding while Kaen laid out the details for the first iteration of the plan to take out the Trol ship. When he got to the part about the TK weapon not working, Olvera's composure broke.

"It *what*?!" she exclaimed, her eyes bugging out. "Sorry, sir, it's just…"

"I know, I haven't been able to make proper sense of it myself. But we are about to implement a plan to disable those countermeasures, which we're hopeful will allow us to use the weapon. If we can't for whatever reason, though, we'll need a way to keep Guard operations and the ships' computers from being hacked again, to ensure we have a secure command center from which to lead our counterattack."

"Network patches are in progress."

"Is there anything else we can do?" Kaen asked. "I know this is far from my area of expertise, but they've broken through the digital security once. Are those patches a certain fix?"

Olvera was silent for a moment. "You're right. We were approaching this from a 'this *should* work' standpoint rather than reengineering the system to make it a surety."

"My guess is you don't have time for a complete overhaul."

"No, we definitely don't—at least not before that ship hits the Elvar Trinary."

"Any ideas, or are we in wait-and-see mode?"

She sighed and shook her head. "Sir, I wish more than anything I could offer a solution that would set our minds at ease. Truth is, though, they got their hands on some of our best tech. The Guard on its own doesn't have the resources to implement long-term safeguards. The system needs to be rebuilt from scratch, and that will take the original AI programmers significant time to complete, if we go that route."

"In other words, taking out the enemy is our only viable security measure," Kaen concluded.

"Yes, sir, that is my professional opinion. Otherwise, if they come for us, there's not much we'd be able to do to stop them."

He scoffed. "The perfect storm of components to hit all our vulnerabilities at once."

"And, to be clear, those weak points are *very* minor. Our security was designed to keep out the kind of enemies we know. Trols don't operate like them. When they got access to that external processor, we gave them the keys to the backdoor."

Blowing up Gaelon was supposed to take care of that

problem. Are there more of them out there besides this one ship?

Kaen nodded. "I'll leave you to finishing the patches, then. After we get through this successfully, we can work on that overhaul."

"Yes, sir. We'll do our best."

Kaen ended the call and then swiveled around to stare out the viewport in his temporary quarters aboard the *Conquest*.

The alien planet-ship appeared no larger than a fist at their pursuit range, a dull gray sphere against the velvet blackness. Aside from its size, it didn't look like much—maybe an industrial colony ship, but certainly not the potential system-killer that it was.

When he thought about the threats facing the Empire, Kaen's biggest concern had always been a massive fleet augmented by armored foot soldiers. Perhaps venturing from another galaxy, this foe, in his nightmares, would present an overwhelming force the Empire would have no way of defeating. His imaginings had always led to the Empire and the enemy fleet squaring off against one another, but he didn't know if they'd fight until the bitter end or find another solution.

The Trols defied that worst-case scenario vision. This was a single, massive ship, capable of travel from system to system within the Taran realm, capable of wiping out those worlds.

He wouldn't admit it to anyone, but Kaen was terrified that their preparations would be for nothing. Any ship capable of negating a pure energy beam from the TK weapon would certainly be able to cut through planetary shields. No matter what protective tech they gave the worlds in the Elvar Trinary, it was only for show. Something to make them feel better— something to give them hope.

In reality, the alien ship could level everything that Tarano had been working so hard to build.

Kira has to succeed.

Kaen hated to put pressure on one individual, but it all came down to the ensuing hours. If the mission failed, they'd be in serious trouble.

— — —

"This is nuts, right?" Leon said to his team. "I mean, communicating with a bunch of dust?"

"No and no," Jack replied. "Actually, I feel pretty dumb now." He pulled his hands out from the rubber gloves in the glove box containing the sample vials of Gaelon debris.

"I'd think you'd be used to that state." Tess smirked.

Jack playfully narrowed his eyes. "Sure, laugh all you want, but you didn't think of it, either."

Leon raised an eyebrow. "What are you talking about?"

"All the assessments we've been doing for the last month. We were testing for the wrong things," Jack replied.

"Please, enlighten me." Leon crossed his arms.

Jack flourished his hand. "Well, for starters, we were focused on where the debris was from—cross-referencing mining records, radiation patterns, and the like. The entire time, we assumed the material was *dead*."

Leon's brow knitted. "It's… rock."

"Wrong!" Jack declared triumphantly, pointing his right index finger into the air. "This entire time, the material was something other than what we thought. Each one of those little granules is part of a linked system. They may have started out as raw rock fragments, but they've been imbued with a unique electromagnetic resonance connection. When that signal ran through the station, the fragments remembered what they used to be in the dwarf planet and were trying to rebuild it. However, as soon as the signal went away, they returned to their dormant state."

"How does that conversion process happen, from raw mineral to... whatever these things are?" Leon asked.

"Beats me." Jack shrugged. "Ultimately, it's irrelevant. What matters is that we now know that every little granule here has the ability to communicate with others of its kind."

Leon perked up. "Great! That means Kira doesn't have to go inside that thing to establish a connection."

Jack winced. "Not exactly. I said 'communicate with', not that any given point could act as a transmitter."

Tess nodded. "The materials are different, but it's still part of a larger collective. Just because the cells in our bodies work together, that doesn't mean all of them can independently relay sensory feedback."

"Okay, so we still need to tap into the brain," Leon surmised, wishing he hadn't let himself get temporarily hopeful.

"Not the brain, necessarily, but at least a nerve," Jack continued. "Working with these granules will let us learn how to speak the language—building on the frequency patterns we recorded while they were active before, we can see if the particles respond when we feed it data. However, once we figure out how to talk to them, we'll still need a connection to a central node that has a direct link to the other components."

"And how do we identify one of those nodes on the ship?" Leon prompted.

"There should be a reaction," Tess jumped in. "The entire purpose of this mission is to disrupt the ship's systems, not make friends with it, right? All we'd have to do is feed it some poison. If the reaction is localized, the particles will just be filler material. But, if the effects of that poison are observable elsewhere, it's tapped into a 'nerve'. Once that location is identified, Kira will know where to plant the hacking tool."

Leon looked between the two techs. "Sounds great, but if each of these particulates have some degree of smarts and they can move around into different shapes, how do we make sure the hacking equipment stays connected? The ship could just spit it out."

"Uh…" Jack scratched his head.

"We could disguise it," Tess suggested. "If we can isolate what makes the particles appear dormant and disconnected, maybe we can give the hacking gizmo a skin that will make the ship think it's just another component."

"That sounds awesome. But how?" Leon asked.

"Frequency patterns," Jack said, getting a distant look in his eyes. "Hold on, I think I have an idea."

He ran back to his work console and started making furious entries on the desktop.

"Should I be doing anything?" Tess asked tentatively.

"Probably best to let him work," Leon replied. While his own skillset had certainly broadened in recent weeks, this wasn't a job for a geneticist or a xenobiologist.

Leon and Tess returned to their own stations while Jack worked on whatever brilliant solution had come to him. After twenty minutes, the researcher finally pushed back from his desk.

"Stars, I'm good."

"All right, Jack, tell us how amazing you are," Tess said with an exaggerated eyeroll.

"Well," Jack grinned, "I went over the frequency patterns we've observed across various media. While many of the signals *appeared* to be the same as in our prior analysis, there were… undertones to some of them, which were only apparent when looking at the signals together. I cross-referenced those against the *Conquest*'s sensor data, and I believe I've devised three signals that will interact with the engineered structures within the alien vessel.

"The first is, essentially, a 'don't-mind-me' signal, like the general matter puts off. I think we can use this to disguise the hacking device so the ship doesn't see it as a threat.

"The second frequency is a counter-wave that should function like a poison. It's not an exact opposing frequency to break apart the structure, but it will disrupt the bonds. Kira can use this to trace the nerve fibers. I believe this would also be an effective frequency to use in the skin of Kira's suit, so they can't grab her."

"Question," Tess said, partially raising her hand. "If we charge Kira's suit with a frequency that disrupts the bonds like that, wouldn't she, you know, fall through the floor?"

Jack frowned. "That could be a problem, yeah."

"But maybe not at a lower intensity," Leon jumped in. "If it was set to more of a 'pulse' rather than a constant, it could keep her from sinking into the ground without them being able to grab her."

"Better yet, if the intensity could be modulated around zones of her suit—pulsing on the bottom of her feet, but stronger above," Tess added.

Jack nodded. "It could work, but that would take some time to configure."

"Then we still have more work to do," Leon stated. "What was the final element? You said there were three."

"Only our all-access pass." Jack beamed. "I located the communication channel. It's similar to the background hum we observed in Gaelon but with some slight variation—like a dialect. Activate that baby, and it should give the hacking team an open backdoor into the central operating system of the ship." When he concluded, he folded his hands in his lap, still grinning.

Leon blinked twice. "I don't know what to say."

"He's fishing for a compliment," Tess advised. "I have to admit, despite acting like an ass most of the time, you do have a stroke of genius in you, Jack."

"Really good work. It would have taken me forever to figure that out, if ever," Leon added. "Thank you."

Jack bowed in his chair. "Glad to be of service."

"All right, let's give the *Conquest* an update, and then we need to figure out how to make those signals work as a suit skin," Leon said. *Hopefully it will be enough to keep Kira safe.*

CHAPTER 13

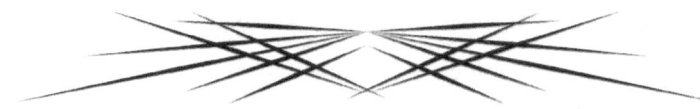

"SHITE, DID YOU get that report from the north polar station?" Trisha said, running into Ellen's office.

"Just saw it in my inbox," Ellen replied. She pulled up the message from Eric, the Mysaran government liaison assigned to the station:

>>Onsite maintenance crew refuses to cooperate with installation. Please advise.<<

"Ugh." Ellen slouched in her chair. "Have you tried calling?"

"I thought you'd want to be on that."

"Trisha," Ellen sat up straighter and folded her hands on the desktop, "you know these issues as well as I do. You don't need my permission."

"I wasn't sure what to suggest," the other woman replied.

"What do your instincts tell you to do?"

"Have a video call with the station manager. If he won't see reason, then politely excuse him from his duties. However, if it comes to that, his staff might feel the same way. Some backup muscle may be needed."

Ellen nodded. "Given that, how do we proceed?"

"Conduct the call to evaluate the severity of the situation. If there's still conflict, send a military unit to facilitate future discussions."

"Except…"

Trisha took a deep breath. "No one can know why we're doing this or why it's so important."

"So, how do we proceed?" Ellen asked again.

This was Trisha's test, whether she realized it or not. There was no better opportunity for Ellen to see how she handled pressure than to throw her straight into the fire.

Ellen was surprised at her own handling of the situation. She'd encountered her share of crises over the years, but nothing even close to the scale of looming planetary annihilation. When it came down to it, though, there were common elements to every problem. A secret was a secret, orders were orders, and a timeline was a timeline. The magnitude of risk may change, but she was used to meeting critical deadlines—even if past stakes had only been getting a file uploaded in time for the morning news.

Trisha was newer to the crunch, but she had a good head on her shoulders. Ellen waited for her to arrive at the logical conclusion for their specific situation.

"If we do need to call in military support," Trisha continued after several seconds, "we need to only explain who needs to be detained. We have a representative onsite who can provide more details at their discretion."

"Exactly." Ellen smiled. "See? You don't need me."

"Will you still sit in on the call? I think it would carry more weight to have an Empire representative present."

"Of course, but you should lead the discussion. I'll only

jump in if necessary," Ellen agreed. *I don't think my younger self would even recognize my new willingness to delegate! Not that the actual conversation will necessarily go that way.*

"I'll get it set up. My office in five minutes." Trisha rushed down the hall.

While she waited, Ellen quickly checked in with Edgar at one of the shield stations on the equator. Despite a smooth start to the project, his latest report had three items flagged in red and two in yellow, indicating issues encountered with the installation checklist.

Great.

She called Edgar.

"You just got my report, didn't you?" he asked by way of greeting.

"What happened? I thought you were already past those points in the installation."

"Yeah, we were," Edgar replied. "We got the equipment in place just fine, but our system won't talk to it."

"We tested for that. It was fine."

"What can I say? Technology. It worked in the tests, but it doesn't work in the field."

"Well, shite." Ellen's face flushed. "You're the furthest along of any of the stations, so this is about to become a system-wide issue."

"I figured as much."

"Do the Guard techs have any ideas?" she asked.

"They have some sort of software patch in mind, but one of the techs objected, saying that it may be compromised. When I pressed, they didn't elaborate."

"That sounds bad."

"Doesn't it? Not sure if a software security issue is better than no shield."

Ellen shook her head. "Not no shield. We do have one already, even though it's not designed to repel heavy weapons."

"Should I tell them to forget it?"

"Hold on, I'm thinking." Ellen rubbed her eyes.

The physical components fit—that was definitely the trickiest part. The matter of having two computer systems talk to each other wasn't an insurmountable barrier. If the only way to have the two systems integrate was a patch that would leave the system vulnerable to potential security issues, then there needed to be some kind of intermediary system that would enable the integration without the security risks.

"We need a translator," Ellen stated.

"This isn't a language barrier issue—"

"No, I mean for the computers. We need a third system that can talk to both of them, but that has a firewall to mitigate the security concerns."

Edgar's eyes lit up with understanding. "Okay, yes, that might work. But I have no idea how to do that thing you just described."

"Neither do I, but between MTech and the university, there has to be a computer expert somewhere who can figure it out."

"I imagine so, but—"

"I'm late for another meeting. Get started on researching some local experts in the industry. I imagine it's a very short list."

"All right," he agreed.

"I can help you reach out as soon as I'm done with this other discussion," Ellen said. "Good luck."

She hung up before he could think of another question to which she didn't have an answer.

Her mind switched back to the issue with the north polar shield station. If they were already having difficulty getting the techs to agree to the equipment installation, trying to sell a software interface was going to be even harder. At least now she knew about the issue before entering the discussion.

Ellen raced down the hall to Trisha's office and found that the call was already underway. She slipped through the door as quietly as possible.

"Ellen Calleti, the Elusian press secretary and our Empire liaison for this project, has joined us," Trisha introduced as Ellen came into the frame.

"Please excuse my tardiness," she said, taking in the faces of those on the other side of the video call.

To her relief, a digital overlay of translucent nametags were floating above the heads of the three individuals on the screen, stating their name and role. Eric, the government rep dispatched to the station, Ellen knew already. A brunette woman named Gwen was marked as the lead Guard tech for the installation, and the station manager was a scowling man named Bernard.

"So, Bernard," Trisha said, "what seems to be the trouble?"

"It's against policy to accept equipment for installation without a signed order from the Mysaran chancellor."

"I appreciate your dedication to policy, but there *is* no Mysaran chancellor at the moment," she replied. "Eric is functioning as an authorized Mysaran government representative in this matter. His word should be regarded with the weight of an order from the former chancellor."

"My duty is to maintain a secure perimeter for Mysar." Bernard directed a glare at Ellen. "I don't know how an outsider ended up in charge, but I will maintain my directive until a new chancellor is in place to give me updated orders."

Ellen tried to relax her appearance, but she was too tense from thinking about the issue with Edgar for it to change much. "That kind of dedication is admirable, and Mysar is lucky to have you. However, there isn't going to be a new Mysaran chancellor."

Trisha shifted in her seat. "Nothing is decided yet."

"No one wants the job." Ellen shrugged. "It's funny, isn't it? One chancellor dies, and not a single person wants to take over the position. The truth is, Bernard, Mysar has been without a designated leader for the past five weeks. Doesn't instill a lot of confidence in the government, huh? But things haven't fallen apart. The reason it hasn't is because of the great work people like Eric and Trisha are doing.

"If they were behind some devious scheme, working with the Empire to bring Mysar down, they could have carried out any manner of subversive attacks already. Instead, the Empire is offering to upgrade our shields to help keep us safe. Considering that we don't have much of a military, or even a dedicated leader making economic and governance decisions for us right now, I don't think it's wise for us to turn down a gift when it's offered."

The man sat in silence for five seconds, working his mouth. "Did you assassinate the former chancellor so the Empire would come here?"

Ellen scoffed. "No. It was nothing like that."

The official communications about what had happened with Chancellor Hale had been as vague as possible to give answers without revealing the truth. For all most people knew, outside the remaining government leadership and a handful of staff at MTech, the chancellor and other officials had been engaged in subversive activities behind the scenes, conspiring with the Sovereign to transform the world into a dictatorship and launch a civil war within the Elvar Trinary. Most people had accepted the story and taken the side of unity, but a few—

as seemed to be the case with Bernard—were attracted to those separatist ideals and resisted the notion of becoming an Empire world.

There was no evidence Ellen could present that would change Bernard's opinion of Hale; fallen idols had a way of always being infallible. She could, however, maybe show him that the Empire wasn't the evil menace he'd convinced himself it was.

"Do you remember the history of our system?" Ellen asked him.

"Of course. We all learned it in school."

"Then you'll recall that our ancestors came here as independent colonists, but they were all from the Taran Empire. They aren't the enemy; they're our long-lost family."

Bernard wet his lips. "Our ancestors left for a reason. They wanted to get away."

"Did they?" Ellen countered. "Maybe they had a sense of adventure and found themselves way out here on their own. Did they *really* intend to sever ties, or was this location just so remote that they lost touch with the core worlds?"

"Maybe."

Ellen nodded to Trisha. She'd softened him up, but Trisha needed to be the one to drive the argument home.

"The point is, Bernard, that 'insiders', 'outsiders', 'enemy', and 'friend' are subjective terms based on your current perspective," Trisha said. "But I am *certain* that the settlers of this system intended for us to be united across our three worlds. That makes Elusia our friend, and as a member of the Empire, that means the Empire is our friend, too, by extension."

He crossed his arms. "Nice speech, and maybe you do have a point, but that's not the issue at hand. Why are you so insistent about these upgrades?"

"Safety and security," Trisha replied. "I can't say more than that right now, but I give you my assurance as a citizen of this system that the Empire's intentions are honorable. Please, assist the technicians with this installation."

"What happens if my crew and I refuse?"

Trisha folded her hands on the tabletop. "Then you will be removed from your posts by force. I don't want it to come to that, because I feel that would be the start of a civil war. Our people don't need to be torn apart—we need to be united."

He eyed her. "I know there's something you're not telling us."

"I guess we're acting like a real government now, then." Ellen smiled. "You wanted your new chancellor? Well, Trisha here is as close to a political head of state as we have right now. Are you going to listen to her, or do you want to resist and put the people of this world at risk?"

Bernard sighed. "What choice do I have? Install your bomaxed equipment."

"Thank you." The tension went out of Trisha. "You won't have any reason to regret this."

"I hope not." Bernard rose from the table. "I guess we have a lot of work to do."

"Yes," Eric agreed. "Gwen, let us know how we can help."

The video feed ended as the team at the polar station got to work.

"Well done," Ellen told Trisha.

"Me? You did a lot of the talking."

More than I intended. So much for keeping my mouth shut. Ellen smiled. "You closed the deal."

She lit up. "I guess I did, didn't I?"

"I knew you could do it." Ellen glanced toward the door.

"You have everything under control. I need to attend to some other matters."

Trisha's face drained. "What's going on?"

"Oh, that new tech we just convinced them to install won't do a bomaxed thing unless we devise a new interface between the software systems."

"What?!"

"Hey, I never said this would be simple."

CHAPTER 14

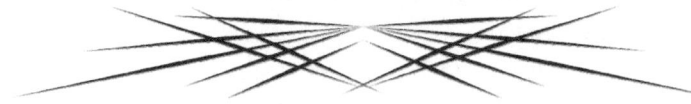

<THE RAVEN *JUST arrived,>* Jasmine informed Kira in her mind.

<Almost go time.>

Kira felt energized after the sparring session with Jason and her subsequent practice of the new skills he'd taught her. Getting to stretch her legs, both in a literal and figurative sense, was a welcome change from being cooped up in her cabin.

She tried to keep her mind off the mission ahead by thinking about how powerful her new abilities made her feel. Dashing across a cargo bay in a split second made for good fun, but getting to fight back against an enemy threatening her home would bring an even greater sense of satisfaction.

<Are you nervous?> Jasmine asked. *<I'm surprised you aren't showing more physiological signs of stress.>*

<I'm excited, if anything. Yeah, it's scary, but we get to be the first ones to go inside a ship from stars know where. That's pretty incredible.>

<Yes, that's true. The scientist part of me is fascinated to see

what we can learn, but that's overshadowed somewhat by the statistical odds of something going terribly wrong.>

<I thought you knew by now that your 'models of doom' aren't helpful—or even accurate. Based on how often you think I'm about to get turned into a pile of goo, shouldn't it have already happened by now?>

<That's what worries me. The odds will catch up eventually.>

<Or you need to add in some new variables,> Kira countered. <You consistently neglect one critical factor.>

<What's that?>

<Determination. Heart. Whatever you want to call it. You can stack the odds against me all you want, but I'll always beat them.>

Jasmine chuckled. <You're right. I need to add 'the Kira factor' into the equation.>

<Make sure that makes it into an official report somewhere. It has a nice ring to it.>

While a shuttle from the Raven docked in the Conquest's hangar, Kira made the trek to the belly of the ship so she could greet her team.

Kira entered on a mezzanine at the midpoint of the room. Rows of fighters covered a third of the massive hangar's deck, and racks of spare parts were suspended in a complex storage scheme near the overhead. Technicians were locking the shuttle's final docking tethers into place. Two dozen additional workers were standing by at various stations throughout the hangar.

Seeing them at their posts, Kira realized that the ship was on alert—ready for battle. She'd been almost exclusively in her cabin or training in the empty cargo bay, so she hadn't noticed the preparations taking place around her.

If I fail, those fighters and this ship are the last line of defense for the Elvar Trinary. With the thought, the reality of what she was about to do really set in.

<Shite, Jasmine, I had to go and think about it.>

<We're going to be fine, Kira. With that new variable added to my model, we now have a ninety-nine point nine percent chance of success.>

Kira frowned in her mind while she descended the stairway to the hangar deck. *<What about the other zero point one percent?>*

<You're a significant factor, my dear, but I'm still a scientist. Nothing is an absolute certainty.>

<All right, fair enough.>

At the bottom of the stairs, Kira jogged to the shuttle.

The side hatch opened, and Ari poked his head out. "Wow, this place is fancy." He spotted Kira. "Oh, hey!"

"Welcome aboard," she greeted with a wave. The uneasiness in her stomach settled a little seeing a familiar face, but not enough to relax her again.

<Want me to adjust your neurochemistry?> Jasmine offered.

<Not now. Maybe some pre-op jitters will be good for me. I think I was starting to feel a little too invincible.>

Nia, Kyle, and Major Sandren followed Ari down the exit ramp. They took in the cavernous hangar with reserved wonder.

"Ma'am, you're out of your mind," Ari said as he approached her.

"Missed you, too." She smiled back. "I know this plan is a little out there, but that's how we roll."

"Aside from the part about you going in alone," Kyle replied, crossing his arms.

"I still don't like it one bit," Nia added.

Behind them, Sandren cleared his throat. "I believe we have a briefing to attend?"

"Sorry, sir." Ari headed for the hangar exit on the deck level.

Kira fell into pace next to Sandren at the back of the group as they headed for the door. "Thank you for believing in me, sir," she said.

"You really shouldn't be thanking me. My endorsement of this plan doesn't mean I like it. But, I respect any soldier who would volunteer to put their life on the line like this. We have a high bar for what constitutes the call of duty, but you're exceeding even that."

"I kind of have to. I'm the only one who we know can go in there."

"You are, but that doesn't change the courage required to rise to the occasion."

"All in a day's work, sir." She smiled.

"You're a fine officer, Kira. You'll have a great future here in the Guard."

Assuming I make it out of this alive. The thought was intended to be private, but Jasmine must have picked up on her shift in mood.

<We're going to do this, Kira. It's scary, but it's not impossible. We have the best people to help us succeed.>

<You're right. We've got this.>

Kira and Sandren caught up with the rest of the team, and she led them to the conference room where Kaen was waiting to brief them with Jason.

The room was situated on the outer bulkhead of the ship, and an expansive viewport offered a terrifying view of the alien ship.

Ari stopped in his tracks as soon as he saw it. "Holy fok," he whispered under his breath.

"Yeah, it's big," Kira whispered back.

"That's an understatement." Nia shook her head. "It looks like a normal ship from here, but I know we're nowhere close to it."

They team did a second double-take when they saw the young TSS Agent captain of the ship.

"Jason Sietinen," he greeted. "Welcome aboard the *Conquest*."

"You're…" Nia faded out.

"Please take your seats," Colonel Kaen stated. He sat in the chair at the head of the table.

Kira quickly found her seat on the far side of the table next to Jason, facing the door—leaving the side facing the viewport for her teammates. She'd already had her fill of looking at the enemy target.

"We've had a number of teams working on various components of this plan, and it's time all the pieces come together," the colonel began. "We are the core team. Kira will be inside the enemy ship, Agent Sietinen will be in command of the *Conquest* with me functioning as a Guard liaison, and the rest of you will be on the *Raven*, hacking the alien ship.

"The plan is relatively straightforward. The *Raven*, being smaller and with stealth capabilities, will approach the enemy vessel and maintain active signal cancellation to prevent the Trols from gaining control of the ship or crew. Kira will take a stealthed shuttle from the *Raven* and dock with the alien vessel. She will then proceed inside to plant a backdoor in the first node with ship-wide communication she can identify, which the team on the *Raven* will use to hack in and disable the alien ship's defenses. The *Conquest* will then fire the TK weapon to destroy the target.

"Of course, executing the individual parts of that plan will be challenging. The purpose of this meeting is to identify and fill in the gaps in our tactics."

When he concluded, Kaen looked around the table. "This is an open discussion; please speak freely. The first matter for us to discuss is the point of ingress." He brought up a holographic model of the alien sphere. "Ideas?"

"I think it needs to be near that collection of towers," Kira said. "I've been over the model several times, and three potential access points have jumped out. The first is here." She glided her finger across the touch-surface desktop to rotate and zoom the image, focusing on a shadowed area at the base of the central tower. "You can't see it very well in this image, but there's what looks like a hangar bay entrance here in the shadows. There's a smaller doorway that I could bring the shuttle through."

"Question." Kyle's hand shot up. "Is there atmosphere in this thing? Are you going in an EVA suit or powered armor?"

"Uh…" Kira glanced at Kaen and Sandren. "I was going to get to that later, but I think I need to go in some light body armor. There *is* a breathable atmosphere inside—similar to the dwarf planet. The new abilities I've been practicing are better than what I could do in powered armor. It would just hold me back."

"You intend to be in the Robus state for this mission?" Kaen asked.

"Not while I need to do precision work with my hands, of course, but movement will be a lot faster in that form."

He nodded. "I suspected you'd suggest as much. Jasmine will need to monitor your vitals for any sign of contagion, but there are distinct advantages to going in without a closed suit."

"I'll be on high alert," Jasmine acknowledged over the audible comms.

"So, not having a suit," Kira continued, "I need a place to set down inside, or where I can get a seal. That first location I pointed out offers a direct way inside, but going into a massive hangar might not be the best approach.

"That's why I identified this second option." She rotated the image again, this time to a recess at the base of one of the outlying towers. "Each of these secondary towers offers direct access deeper into the ship, based on our scan data. *This* one, though, and the one opposite, also have corridors leading to the central tower. Twenty-three kilometers beneath that central tower is the chamber containing a node like we saw on Gaelon."

"With the interface Leon's team developed, you won't have to go all the way down there," Sandren interjected. "But finding a corridor that connects to the central node will almost certainly give you the right channel to tap into."

She nodded. "Looking at those design specs is what gave me the idea. My initial thought was I needed to find the most direct route to physically get to the center, but that design should enable me to stay relatively close to the surface."

"My concern with the entire plan is that we can't fire until you're clear from the alien ship after the equipment is in place," Jason spoke up. "We may not have a very long window between gaining access and when they figure out how to block us again."

"And the deeper I go, the longer it will take to get out. Yeah, I know." Kira sighed. "That's what led me to the third option."

Jason tilted his head. "Which is?"

"I take the shuttle in through one of the cylinders. The top is open to space, but the artificial gravity holds atmosphere inside at the bottom, just like on a planet. I can take the shuttle down and be close to the core without having to worry about docking doors and all that. Being closer to the shuttle also means I could make a faster escape after the equipment is in place."

"A quick exit is critical," Kaen stated. "I don't like the idea of you being near so many of those 'pits', or 'nests'—whatever they are—but the logistics of that location make the most sense."

Kira inclined her head. "I agree, sir."

"With the access point established, the only remaining preparation is testing the frequency generators for Kira's suit and the hacking module. Any questions before we adjourn?" The colonel looked around the table.

"How long will it take us to get clear of the blast zone?" Sandren asked.

"Based on the planned holding distance from the alien ship and the *Raven*'s maximum acceleration, you will need a minimum of three minutes and twenty-seven seconds to clear the lethal range of the TK weapon's blast," Jasmine replied over the comm.

The major nodded. "We'll call it four minutes to be safe. We'll need to time it just right, so the hack corresponds with the time we're at a safe range."

"That will be nearly impossible to plan, but we'll do our best," Nia said.

"Any other thoughts?" Kaen asked.

Ari raised his hand. "After we beat these guys, do we get another party?"

<See? Told you cake is an excellent motivational tool,> Kira said to Jasmine.

<I stand corrected.>

Kaen chuckled. "I think we can arrange something. Dismissed," he said to the attendees, but nodded toward Kira to indicate she should stay.

His eyes met hers as the last team member left the room. "I would be remiss in my command duties if I didn't ask you one last time: are you sure about this?"

"Absolutely," she replied without hesitation. "I trained for this. I'm ready."

Kaen rose from the table. "Very well. Let's begin."

CHAPTER 15

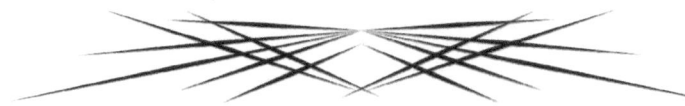

"YOU'RE REALLY GOING in only wearing *that*?" Kyle asked while eyeing Kira's light armor.

She grinned back. "Isn't it stylish?"

"Fashion isn't my reason for asking."

Ballistic padding covered her torso, elbows, and knees, but the rest of her was completely exposed, aside from the minimal protection offered by her shipsuit. To freely transform to her Robus state and back, the flexible attire was necessary.

Kira patted Kyle on his shoulder. "I appreciate your concern, but there aren't big scary guys with guns inside this ship. The dust particles won't be able to get me with the charged suit skin, whether it's powered armor or this stuff."

"All the same, you're bringing your sidearm," Sandren said.

She smiled. "I'd never think of going anywhere without it."

Nia stood up from the console where she'd been working. "All right. Let's give this a test run." She shooed everyone away from Kira. "I apologize in advance if the intensity isn't right."

An electric shock ignited Kira's skin. "Ow!"

The sensation of jabbing needles receded, but she still sensed a lingering charge.

"Whoopsy." Nia blushed. "Overdid it there a little."

"I take it you weren't *trying* to electrocute me." Kira rubbed her hands along her forearms in an attempt to diminish the strange tingling sensation.

"The charge needs to be strong enough to flow through the entire suit without being so strong as to do *that*," Nia replied. "Getting an even intensity across all zones is tricky."

"Ever thought of starting low and ramping up?" Kira looked at her friend from under her brow.

"Yeah, well, if you're so tough now, you can take it." Nia smirked. "Let's try this."

Another charge tickled Kira's skin, but it was more of a background hum.

"I can definitely tolerate this level," she reported.

"Coverage looks good," Kyle observed from a station next to Nia's. "Let's see how that plays with the module."

The device they'd constructed for the remote hack was a black box the size of Kira's two hands. A prong on one side would serve as a physical jack, which would offer a more secure connection than tapping in through the wireless network. To keep the ship from expelling the foreign device, its shell would be charged with the same frequency as Kira's suit.

Unfortunately, they would have no assurances that the countermeasure worked until they were on board the ship.

Kyle hooked the test equipment up to the device, powered it on, and then returned to his computer.

"Charge looks to be evenly distributed and holding," he reported.

"Fingers crossed." Nia disconnected the device. She

handed it to Kira for her to stow in her cross-body satchel.

"There's also this," Kyle said, grabbing a similar-looking device from his desktop. It was half the size of the main module. "This is a signal booster, of sorts. You shouldn't need it, but you can place it in a central location as a signal relay if we're unable to connect directly with the main device."

"Got it." Kira placed it in her bag next to the module. "Anything else?"

"Don't die," Ari advised.

"My number one checklist item," she said, miming the action of marking an imaginary list in front of her.

"Then we're all set," Kyle said with a smile, but she could see the worry in his eyes—in everyone's eyes.

"I'll be fine," she assured them. "Back before you know it."

Nia ran over and gave her a hug. "Good luck."

"Thanks. Let's head out."

They gathered their equipment and climbed aboard the shuttle to head back to the *Raven*. Once they docked on the other ship, Kira remained in the shuttle while the others went to their stations.

From the shuttle's cockpit, she watched Kyle, Nia, and Ari set up a workstation in the *Raven*'s bay using equipment appropriated from the *Conquest*. Meanwhile, Sandren went to observe the activities from the bridge with Rodrick and Aleya.

Kira tapped into the video feed from the *Raven*'s helm on a holographic overlay of the shuttle's front viewport.

<*How are you doing with all this, Jasmine?*>

<*Feeling as confident as I ever will. It's times like this when it's beneficial to not be beholden to emotions in the way you are. I can be objective about the mission.*>

< *Ah, 'the mission'! How far you've come in just a few weeks. Before, you were all about your science labs.*>

<A new universe has been opened to me. I think being in your mind has made me a vicarious adrenaline junkie.>

<It is rather addictive.>

The view depicted on the holographic overlay in front of the shuttle's viewport shifted as the *Raven* swung around to face the alien ship.

They sped toward it. At first, the alien sphere didn't appear to be getting much larger. As they neared, however, it rapidly grew. Horizontal and vertical bands became more distinct. Though it had appeared to be relatively dull from a distance, there were actually tiny lights dotting the structure.

<What kind of illumination is that? Are those ports?>

<No, I think it's glowing,> Jasmine replied.

<The same kind of bioluminescence as in the pits?>

<I believe so, but…> Jasmine uncharacteristically faded out. *<Given the distance we still are from the vessel, each of those points of light is a kilometer or more in diameter. I don't know what they might be.>*

When the alien ship took up the entire viewport, the *Raven* dipped toward the alien ship's southern pole, relative to their approach vector.

"Comm check?" Kyle said in Kira's earpiece.

"Loud and clear," she replied.

"Confirmed," Jasmine added. *<And double-checked,>* she added as a non-spoken communication over the link.

<You can relay my thoughts, right?> Kira checked with her.

<Yes, if you think something to me, I can pass it on.>

<That might be better than us talking out loud.>

<Agreed.>

The *Raven* neared the southern pole, closing in on the location of one of the massive cylinders embedded in the alien ship.

"Thirty seconds until departure," Sandren said over the comm. "May the stars be with you."

"See you soon, sir."

Jasmine set a countdown clock on the shuttle's HUD, and Kira took several slow, deep breaths.

At zero, the shuttle dropped from the *Raven*'s belly through the force field. Once in the vacuum, the shuttle's engines kicked in, and it sped toward the narrow entry to the alien ship at the top of the target cylinder.

Rather, it had appeared narrow from a distance. As the shuttle approached, the scale of the alien ship hit her full force. Tiny specks on holographic models were now two-kilometer chasms, and the larger features were the size of continents.

<How the fok did they build this thing?>

<Like their other structures—they grew it,> Jasmine replied. *<They must have mined multiple worlds to make this one, given the uniformity of the elements. You can't find these concentrations on one planet.>*

<I can only hope they weren't inhabited.>

<Best not to think about it. Focus on the fact that this ship won't be able to hurt anyone else.>

The end of the cylinder was a cap suspended two kilometers above the main surface of the ship. It had appeared dark inside from a distance, but Kira now saw a subtle blue glow coming from within.

<Stars, I hear them!>

Voices washed over her—the same cacophony she had experienced in her first telepathic attempt. Only, the song had changed. Curious and ethereal before, it was now dark and bent on destruction. The Trols were hunting, and the Elvar Trinary was their prey.

As the shuttle entered the ship, milllions of minds turned

their attention to Kira.

"*You cannot hide from us,*" they said. "*Your ship is masked, but we see you.*"

A chill gripped her chest. <*Fok, Jasmine, there are so many of them!*>

<*Don't listen. They can't touch you. Taunting is all they have.*>

"*Such a waste of a mind. You think you can stop us, but there is nothing you can do,*" they sneered.

"*Nice try, but I know exactly what I'm doing.*"

The chorus continued to pester the back of her consciousness, but she blocked out the voices and did her best to focus on the shuttle's progress.

The diameter of the cylinder spanned ten kilometers. Kira wouldn't have been able to see the sides if it wasn't for the distinctive blue glow that looked almost like polka dots in the dark. As they got deeper inside, she realized that each of those dots was actually the top of one of the rock core 'pits' they had observed on the planets, which were slotted into racks on a forty-five degree angle. The racks around the cylinder weren't all filled, but there were at least two dozen of the pits so far in the structure.

Though the Trols didn't have physical eyes, she felt like they were watching her as the shuttle descended past each.

At the bottom of the massive cylinder, the HUD displayed the presence of an oxygen and nitrogen atmosphere, now thick enough to be within breathable tolerances. Noticing that more of the pits were slotted into the racks where the atmosphere was thicker, she speculated that perhaps the Trols thrived on that mixture themselves.

Twenty kilometers down, the shuttle came to rest on the deck of the cylinder, sinking slightly into the groundcover.

<What is this?> she asked Jasmine.

<It looks to be a substance similar to the moss-like material we observed on the Gaelon dwarf planet.>

<I guess it's time to find out if I really can breathe this air, huh?>

<I detect no reason why you wouldn't be able to. And believe me, I am being very conservative in my analysis. The whole sharing a body thing, you know.>

<It does bring me peace of mind that you have a vested interest in keeping me alive.>

<I don't envy the decontamination you'll have to go through after this, just in case, but that skin buffing will give you a great glow for the celebration party.>

<Yay, I think?> Kira rose from the pilot's chair and headed to the back hatch of the shuttle.

<Not to pressure you, but we are on a ticking clock here… and we're not sure when time will run out.>

<I know.> Kira took one final, calming breath. *<Let's do this.>*

She hit the release on the back hatch.

The door lowered to the soft ground. Kira descended it, scoping out her surroundings. Jasmine fed a mental overlay to her, functioning like a HUD without the need for a helmet.

<There isn't that oppressive hum that messed with my head on Gaelon,> Kira observed.

<I believe the frequency surrounding your suit is neutralizing it. However, I'm cancelling out the remaining effects.>

<Just don't dial it back as much as you did last time.>

<Don't worry, I'm not,> Jasmine assured her. *<The passageway we need is to the left.>*

<Got it.> Kira spotted the opening seventy meters away.

She took a moment to look upward at the expansive cylinder around her. She was but a tiny speck in the mammoth enclosure. Space was twenty kilometers above her, and the *Raven* was four minutes away at maximum thrust. She was alone.

Not alone. There's Jasmine, and I have my mission.

Kira transformed into her Robus state while she dashed toward the passageway.

The practice on the *Conquest* had honed her understanding of her new body. As her legs pumped her across the spongy ground, she knew precisely how far and how fast she could run without needing to rest. She could go a long way, and she'd need all of that stamina to make it through the mission.

The passage appeared to be made of stone, like the corridors from Gaelon. The dull, dark material was smooth, yet had a rippled pattern running its length.

As she neared it, the stone began to disintegrate into a cloud.

<Oh, shite, here we go!>

<Suit is active, and there's a shield around the shuttle. Keep moving.>

Kira headed straight into the swarm.

The particles looped around her, trying to latch on, but they were knocked back each time. A one-centimeter-thick air pocket surrounded her entire body. The particles were so close to her eyes that she had to resist the urge to keep swatting them away, but they couldn't come any closer. She was protected.

Kira ran full speed down the passageway, jumping over obstacles as the floor and walls shifted around her. It was too dark to see clearly as she followed Jasmine's map in her mind, so she activated a light that was affixed to the front of her armor. The light cast a blue halo in front of her, illuminating the particle swarm that kept following her, undeterred by the field that kept them at bay. They made it almost impossible to see, so she relied on sensor data from Jasmine.

Two hundred meters down the passage, Kira reached an intersection. *<Which way?>*

<Hmm,> Jasmine floundered.

<What is it?>

<This layout doesn't match the map.>

CHAPTER 16

<WHAT DO YOU mean it doesn't match the map?> Kira demanded. *<I thought the sensor data you used to create it was being gathered in real-time?>*

<Some of the environmental conditions are, yes, but it's being applied to the model that was developed using the Conquest*'s sensors.>*

Kira thought for a moment. *<That was only a couple of hours ago. Why doesn't it match?>*

<There are two potential explanations. The first is that the sensor data was wrong. The second is that things have changed since then.>

<Changed? How would that be possible?>

<If this ship was grown, there is no reason that it would need to stay in one static form.>

<It never changed when we were analyzing it before.>

<There wasn't an invader on board then,> Jasmine pointed out.

<Fok, you're right.> Kira's heart dropped. *<It might be*

shifting around as a strategy to keep us from getting anywhere. It can't stop us because it can't grab us, but it can force us to run in circles.>

<That is the more likely of the two explanations.>

<Shite!>

Kira looked down the two potential paths. Either one was likely to lead them to a dead end. They'd need to find a way to make forward progress somehow.

<I need to tell the Raven what's going on.> She tried to open up a mental comm link. Nothing.

<Jasmine, why can't I connect?>

<Communications appear to be blocked. I can't get through, either.>

<Fok! Then we need to backtrack to the shuttle.> Kira turned around.

The passageway she had just come through was gone.

<Um… that's not good.>

<Uh oh.>

<Not helpful, Jasmine! What do we do? Are we trapped in here?>

<There is always a way, you know that. The first priority is establishing contact with the Raven. We have the signal booster, we just need to figure out where to place it.>

Kira took a calming breath, wishing the particles would stop buzzing around her face for two seconds so she could think in peace. <Okay, if we can't get through to the Raven using our communications equipment in its raw form, then we need to tap into the alien ship.>

<I'm not sure if my systems will be compatible,> Jasmine objected.

<All you need to do is piggyback on a signal connected to the external sensors—I bet even I could do that.>

Jasmine smirked in her mind. *<I see what you're doing...
that was a challenge.>*

<Do you accept?>

<Yes. Head to the right.>

Kira focused on the passageway ahead. *Get to the sensors.
Alert the* Raven. *Destroy the enemy ship. One step at a time.*

— — —

"Any word from the *Raven* or Kira?" Kaen asked the comm
tech seated at a station along the left curvature of the
Conquest's Command Center.

"No, sir."

No news is good news, I suppose. He settled back into his
chair at the center of the room.

"There is something else," Jason spoke up from the seat
next to him. "The alien vessel is almost within range of the
Elvar Trinary's in-system sensor array."

Kaen closed his eyes. *Fok.*

The issue was twofold.

Foremost, the system's residents would be able to see an
approaching planet-sized object. Best-case scenario was they'd
be curious and want to know more; worst-case, there'd be
widespread panic that they were about to die.

A secondary issue was the *Conquest* and its capabilities.
While the TK weapon was infamous in military circles, the
public narrative in recent years had been that the TSS was
demilitarizing. If the residents of the Elvar Trinary witnessed
the engagement with the Trols and saw that the TSS was still in
control of a super-weapon, it would create a PR nightmare—
especially since Mysar and Valta weren't yet officially member
worlds of the Empire.

Kaen didn't want to answer to the TSS and High Dynasties about how such news got out. He needed a solution that would keep the Elvar Trinary safe and would also prevent anyone seeing something they weren't supposed to.

"May I use your office?" Kaen asked Jason.

"Of course. May I ask for what purpose?"

"To call my contact on Elusia. I have an idea for how to address our problem, but I need to get a status update first."

"Understood. We'll be standing by." Jason directed him to the office accessible via the Command Center.

Kaen initiated a call to President Joris as soon as he got settled behind the captain's desk.

The president's face appeared on the viewscreen, looking slightly confused. He relaxed when he saw Kaen. "Colonel, hello! I didn't recognize the credentials on the call."

"Yes, apologies. I'm borrowing office space on a TSS ship. I wanted to check in on the status of the shield installations."

Joris nodded. "It's coming along. We've had some technical barriers to overcome. I believe we're finished with all but one station on Elusia. Valta was delayed due to some… political issues, but we worked through that, and the installation is underway. I believe Mysar is almost complete, as well."

"Do you have a timeline for when it will all be done?"

"Probably twenty minutes for Elusia. I'm not sure about the other worlds. You'd have to ask Ellen."

"I will. Could you forward me her direct contact details on Mysar?"

Momentary surprise flitted across the president's face, but he leaned forward to swipe his hand across his desktop. "Sent."

A notification window popped up on Kaen's screen with the requested information. "Thank you. Now, what was the issue with Valta?"

"There were reportedly some trust concerns regarding the Empire. Again, Ellen was a part of those conversations, not me."

"You've put an awful lot of faith in her."

"She's risen to the occasion. Shocking that she's in this position now, considering she was originally sent to Elusia to kill me, but I've always believed everyone deserves a second chance. The founders of our system came to seek a fresh start, and it's important we honor that legacy."

Now we need to make sure they have a future to build upon. Kaen nodded. "A touching sentiment, and one I agree is important we all remember. Now I need to check in with Ellen."

"Of course. Thank you again for sending the shields. It's set my mind at ease knowing we have an extra layer of protection."

If only he knew how little protection they'll offer against what's headed their way. But that was the power of hope.

"The Empire will gladly protect our own. I'll be in touch if I have any updates." Kaen ended the call.

The last part was a lie. If Kira's mission failed, it was unlikely the *Conquest* would be able to do anything to stop the Trol ship before it reached the system. *Is it better to give warning or to let them live their last moments in peace?* He didn't know the answer.

Setting the dire thought from his mind, he called Ellen on Mysar.

It took thirty seconds for her to pick up. Though he'd never spoken with her before, there was no mistaking the violet-eyed woman as Leon's sister.

"Ellen, I'm Colonel Kaen with the Tararian Guard."

"Oh!" Recognition passed across her face.

"I wanted to check in on the status of your shield upgrades."

"Right, yes." She sighed. "It's been a challenge. First, this one station manager somehow got it in his mind that it was his sole purpose in life to prevent us from installing any Empire tech. We eventually convinced him, but it was a delay. And then we had to solve the interface problem, which set us back again—"

"By how much?"

"No serious delays. We'll be finished with everything in about two hours. So, almost there." She gave a weary smile.

Two hours? The Trol ship will be in visual range before then. Kaen tried not to let his concern show. "Are any of the installations complete?"

"Seven will be within the next half-hour. It's just that north polar one that got pushed back."

"And what about Valta?"

"Half are complete, and I think the others will also be done in about two hours, as well." Her brow knitted. "Why? I thought we had another two days before the ship gets here?"

"You do. And again, it should be disabled well before it ever reaches you. I wanted to make sure everything was proceeding according to plan."

She shrugged. "About as close as anything ever does around here."

"Good, thank you for the update. We'll be in touch soon."

As soon as the call was terminated, he leaned back in the chair and massaged the bridge of his nose. *Will enough of the new shield be active in time?*

He returned to the bridge, where Jason was waiting with a quizzical look.

"Find out what you needed to know?" he asked.

"Yes and no," Kaen replied. "What do you know about planetary shields?"

"They... shield planets," the Agent replied in a tone that sounded more like a question than a statement.

"I have a specific question, if you have a specialist on board."

"Uther in engineering, sir," Rianne chimed in. "We were in the same training cohort. He knows his stuff."

"Thank you. Please open a comm channel to him," Kaen requested.

"Open," the comm tech acknowledged.

"Uther, what would it take to adjust the opacity of a planetary shield?" Kaen asked.

A slight smile touched the corners of Jason's lips as he caught onto the plan.

"Not much, with our current models," the engineer replied over the comm. "They're configured to be able to account for star color spectrum so we can have green vegetation on worlds that otherwise wouldn't support it."

"How many of the nine generators need to be active to sustain a shield?"

"Depends on what you need it to do. For protection, all of them give the best defense. You could probably get away with five of the nine, if it's only a matter of having a field up—to block some minor debris or tint the color."

"Could you make it so people on the surface wouldn't be able to see the sky?"

"Sure, with a little tweaking," the engineer confirmed.

"Good. I have a project for you."

— — —

Ellen frowned at her computer screen. "Strange."

"What is it?" Trisha asked, looking up from the tablet she'd been working on in Ellen's office.

For the past half-hour, they had been going over the final checklist items for the shield installations. All but the north polar station upgrades were complete, and Ellen was ready to call it a night. However, the latest message from the Guard threatened to prolong her already very long day.

"I just got a notice that they're about to push a new software packet out to the shield system," Ellen said. "It says it's some sort of test protocol. We might experience some 'visual disturbance'."

"What does that mean?" Trisha scrunched up her nose.

"Beats me." Ellen brushed her fingertips along her hairline. "I thought we were almost finished."

"Sounds like there's nothing for us to do with this, though. We can sit back and let the Empire do their thing."

Ellen barked a laugh. "If only it was that simple! 'Visual disturbance' means people are going to notice. They'll start asking questions about what's causing it, then we'll need to explain that we took tech from the Empire, and it'll be a landslide from there."

Trisha slumped. "Oh, I didn't think about that part."

"I didn't spend too long in public relations, but what little exposure I did have demonstrated how quickly people will latch onto even the most minor issue. If it's something bigger, we'll have a major incident on our hands."

"Trading one crisis for another." Trisha sighed.

"Welcome to politics."

"We should send out some preemptive alert," Trisha suggested. "If we tell them that we made some shield upgrades, and will be testing out some things, maybe no one will question it if something unusual happens."

"Now you're thinking like a politician," Ellen replied with a smile. "Why don't you draft the communication, and I can review it to add a little extra spin in our favor?"

"Perfect. I'll have you something shortly."

As soon as the other woman was gone, Ellen reread the note from the Guard. *So, there* was *an ulterior motive with that equipment installation, after all.*

A looming physical threat may be one reality, but she suspected that this 'visual disturbance' was an effort to hide something they didn't want citizens to see. Whatever they were covering up, now that the equipment was installed, she had no choice but to trust them.

CHAPTER 17

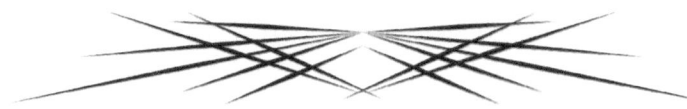

KIRA EYED YET another dark passageway looming before her on the Trol ship. *<Are you sure this is the right way?>*

<You're looking at the same map in your mind that I am. If you have another suggestion, by all means, make it.>

Tensions had been running high as Kira raced through the alien vessel. Just when she felt like they were making progress, she'd realize that they'd gone in a huge circle.

The ship was changing around them. She didn't know when it happened, but one minute a passage would be open to her, and the next it would be gone. While she kept trying to witness it happening to see if there might be a way to stop it, she had yet to be looking in the right place at the right time.

A small blessing, at least, was that the swarm of particles that had been following her when she first entered had finally dissipated. However, a dozen or so specs were still following her movements, perhaps to keep an eye on her. As long as they stayed away from her face, she could ignore them.

<Sorry, Jasmine. This is just really frustrating.>

<I know,> her AI replied, *<but whining won't get us to our destination any faster. We need to get that communication relay in place.>*

That's what I'm trying to do, but these fokers have other plans, she thought to herself.

The fact that even Jasmine was getting the AI-equivalent of anxious had Kira on edge. The mission was supposed to be straightforward: get in, install the tech, and get out. Now she couldn't even chart a path to her destination. She wasn't sure what was worse… that she didn't know the way in, or that she had no idea how to get back out.

The mission comes first.

It was her mantra, and it was even more critical with the fate of her home system on the line—and every system the Trols may visit thereafter. Failure wasn't an option.

Kira halted. *<We need to try something different.>*

<What do you suggest?>

<Have you looked at how the passageway openings are changing? Is there any pattern?>

<Let me see.>

A hum filled Kira's mind as Jasmine's attention was drawn away from cancelling the environmental effects of the Trol ship. The whispers she'd first heard on their approach in the shuttle beckoned at the edge of her consciousness.

<Hmm, it isn't as random as it seemed,> Jasmine said after a minute. *<It appears that sections of the ship are rotating rather than transforming. The sections are on a grid, and those pieces will slide around like a puzzle.>*

<What's the purpose of that?>

<Well, it's proving to be an effective means of keeping an intruder from getting where they are trying to go.>

Kira's heart dropped. *<Or it's directing us to where they*

want us to go.>

<I don't like that hypothesis.>

<Yeah, can't say I do, either.> Kira eyed the three directions she could go from the intersection, one behind and two forward. *<Can you use the movement pattern to our advantage? Can we beat it?>*

<I haven't been able to make a clear determination yet.>

<As long as we stand still, that gives them time to plot against us. We need to keep moving.> If Jasmine wasn't going to make a suggestion, then Kira would need to follow her instincts. And her gut told her to go left—deeper into the ship.

She ran through the mouth of the dark passage, the pool of illumination cast from the light on her suit dancing across the rippled surface. The oppressive quiet, aside from her own footfalls, and the rock-like material all around her gave the impression of being underground in a cave, rather than on a spaceship. Then again, when the ship was the size of a planet, maybe that distinction was meaningless.

The passage opened into a fifteen-meter-diameter cavern with an overhead twice the height of the previous chambers Kira had been inside. Rather than the two-direction fork she was used to seeing, there were three options in addition to the one she had entered from.

In her 'keep moving' efforts, she dashed across the open space, toward the leftmost passage.

<Wait,> Jasmine stopped her. *<There's something different about that direction.>*

<Different is good, right? We want to break this cycle.>

<There are heat signatures I can't explain,> Jasmine said. *<I don't think we should go that way.>*

<Fine, then what do you suggest?>

<Straight ahead. I believe there's a vertical shaft you can

jump down. We need to get to a lower level.>

<Okay,> Kira conceded. She altered her course to head for the passage directly across from where she'd entered the chamber.

The passage narrowed from three meters wide to two after the entry.

<Why does this feel like a funnel of doom?>

<You jest, but...>

<Jasmine!>

<I'm positive we're not walking down the esophagus of a giant space worm, so at least there's that.>

<How very reassur—>

Kira stopped short at the lip of a steep ramp. *<Is this that shaft you were talking about?>*

<The very one,> Jasmine confirmed. *<Good news is that you should be able to easily climb back up, at that angle.>*

<Getting out is a good thing.> Kira peered into the darkness below, shining her light on it as best she could. *<Detect anything that will result in instant-death or impalement if I slide on down?>*

<I don't think so.>

<Jasmine, you need to work on your phrasing.> Kira shifted back, thinking it best that she not have claws to unintentionally poke herself with if she landed hard, and then took the leap.

She skidded down the steep incline along the rippled rock. The frequency generator worked against her; with it keeping the rock from getting any traction on her, she had no friction to slow her down.

By the bottom of the three-story slide, she was going way too fast.

<Oh, shitesnacks.>

The bottom was in sight. She brought her knees to her

chest and pivoted into a horizontal position, tucking her limbs in to roll as soon as she hit the stone floor. She braced for impact.

To her surprise, the slide deposited her on a squishy, fibrous floor similar to the covering on the bottom of the pit where they'd landed the shuttle.

She rose to her feet, unharmed. *<Well, that was convenient.>*
<Um, Kira…>

She snapped her head around to look behind her. Orange glowing eyes were peering out of the shadows in every direction.

<I think I figured out what those heat signatures were on the upper level.>

<Fok, Jasmine! What are these things?> Kira snatched her multi-handgun from its holster, her arms outstretched and ready to fire.

One of the creatures stepped into the pool of light radiating from her suit. Slinking forward on all fours, it was two meters long and stood as high as Kira's chest at its shoulder. The skin was coarse, mimicking the texture of the stone walls, and its four orange eyes bore a similar glow to Kira's own when she was in her Robus state. Its wide jaw was curled back into a menacing snarl, exposing ten-centimeter-long fangs.

<I believe this must be the result of one of the Trols' previous ventures into genetic modification. They made guards for themselves, to stop any fleshy intruders who might make it past their other defenses.>

<Foking perfect.> Kira readied to pull the trigger as the closest creature advanced.

<I don't think that handgun is our best shot here,> Jasmine said. *<You wore that armor for a reason.>*

Kira returned the weapon to its holster. *<You're right, I*

did.>

Adrenaline coursed through her, and she gave into her raw emotion. Silvery nanite claws extended from her own fingertips, and her teeth re-shaped into fangs as sharp and deadly as the ones around her. Shimmering, protective scales covered her exposed skin. She was ready for battle.

Kira dove for the lead creature, slashing her claws across its face. They sliced through the creature's eyes, splattering blood across its rough skin.

<Holy shite! Why haven't I been using these claws in battle all along?!>

<Probably because you normally don't want to eviscerate things.>

<Oh, right, that.>

The lead creature recoiled from Kira's assault, snapping its jaws in a blind attempt to grab her hand.

Kira brought her arm around and raked her claws across its throat.

It yelped in momentary pain, then dropped to the ground, dark blood pouring from its wound.

Another snarl called Kira's attention behind her to her left, and she dove to the side just in time to avoid another creature's lunge for her.

<How many are there?> she asked Jasmine, having not tallied the eyes peering from the darkness.

<With each creature having four eyes, there are eight. That matches the thermal readings from your suit's sensors.>

<Okay, then seven more to go.>

Kira rolled to her back and skewered the second beast as it completed its charge for her. She hurled it to the side as a third joined the fight. The beast snapped at her, spraying spittle in her face as thick saliva oozed from its jowls.

<Guess the suit doesn't repel these guys, too.>

<They're biological, not valteron-permeated minerals like the rest of this structure.>

<What I wouldn't give for a face shield right now!> Kira wiped the back of her left wrist across her slobber-covered face, using her right hand to jab claws into the creature's muscular neck.

It yelped with surprise, recoiling enough for Kira to slip out from under it.

She leaped to her feet and slid her claws down the side of its neck to bleed it out before it could attack again.

<Three down.>

Two more vaulted toward her at the same time, one for her legs and another for her neck. She instinctually turned sideways, and the action of the assault around her crawled to slow motion.

Moving at the edge of the localized spatial distortion, she was able to twist her legs out of harm's way, bringing up her right knee in a powerful thrust to knock the bottom creature off-balance so it would fall into the path of the top assailant.

Her time perception returned to its normal flow, and the two creatures collided with a yelp, just as she'd intended. She was about to finish them off while they were dazed, but searing pain radiated from her left calf.

Kira looked down to find that another creature had darted from the shadows to sink its teeth into her through the nanite scales.

I guess I'm not impervious.

She plunged her claws into the base of the creature's skull, splattering blood across her face. Its jaws opened, and the lifeless form toppled to the side.

The two creatures who'd initially attacked her had

regained their bearings and were rounding on her, while the one remaining beast she had yet to engage stalked her from behind.

Kira faked them out—taking one step forward as though to attack—but she slipped into super-speed just as she ducked, pivoting to go for the one behind her. She slid across the floor and drove her fingers into the creature's chest as it lunged. The carcass continued forward on momentum, offering a shield for Kira. Time perception returned to normal as she twisted back to her feet to face the two creatures charging her.

They leaped over the body without missing a step, their eyes fixed on their prey.

<Duck!>

Kira listened to Jasmine without hesitation.

The creatures had already leaped, unable to change direction midair.

Time slowed down for Kira again as they passed overhead. She brought her hands up and plunged her claws into their sternums, opening them up the entire length of their bellies as they passed overhead. Blood and innards spilled over her in a hideous, dark red wave.

The bodies collapsed on the ground behind her.

Cautiously, Kira rose to her feet, wincing as she put weight on her injured leg. *<Was that all of them?>*

<I don't see anything else on the thermal,> Jasmine replied. *<That was good fighting.>*

Kira looked down at her wound. *<Though I didn't get out unscathed.>*

The puncture wounds from the fangs were deep, but the rest of the damage was superficial. With her upgraded med-nano, the injury wouldn't take long to heal.

<I'll be on the lookout for any more. Can you walk?>

<Yeah, just a flesh wound,> Kira replied while turning to her normal appearance. *<We need to keep moving.>*

She blocked out the carnage around her to assess the layout of the new level. It was a mirror of the chamber she'd been in before the passage leading to the ramp—fifteen meters across, with a total of four passageways, one of which was the ramp.

<Which way?> she asked Jasmine.

<Middle,> the AI replied. *<We're almost to the access point.>*

Kira ran forward as best she could on the injured leg, trying to favor it so it would heal faster.

The middle passage was three meters wide, identical to the other corridors she'd encountered on the strange alien vessel. It extended for nearly one hundred meters before fanning out into a larger cavern with a wave-like rock tower at its center.

<I imagine this is it?> Kira asked the AI.

<It is. Time to see if it's connected to the core of the ship.>

Kira wiped the blood from her hands as best as she could on the outer thighs of her pants, then she reached into her carrying bag to retrieve the signal booster her team had given her.

<Where should I place it?>

<At the base of that central structure, I suppose,> Jasmine instructed. *<If any component in here has tendrils connecting to other parts of the ship, it will be that. I'll trace the signal to see where it leads.>*

Kira put the box in position.

Bits of rock tried to rise up over it, but the rock disintegrated into particles as soon as it made contact with the tuned shield around the device.

<It's still so weird to see the rock move like that,> she said to Jasmine.

<I wish we had a safe way to study this lifeform. It's a unique wonder.>

<It is. The murdery impulses are a major problem, though.>

<I can't disagree with that.> Jasmine paused. *<Hmm.>*

Kira sighed. *<I have come to associate that vocalization with bad things.>*

<Well, it's not good.> Jasmine was quiet for another three seconds. *<Rather, there is* some *good news. The tracer signal Leon's team likened to 'poison' does work. I've been able to trace the network conduits linking this node to the rest of the ship. Unfortunately, it doesn't connect to the core operating module that controls the defenses.>*

<I thought we were just going to this one so we could send a message to the Raven?>

<Yes, though I had hoped we might get lucky. The worse news is that this node doesn't connect to the communications systems, either.>

Kira's blood pressure rose. *<Then what the fok* does *it do?!>*

<I'm working on that. Nothing about this ship is as predicted. I need a few more minutes—there's a lot of data to process.>

<So, we're trapped and still have no way to communicate.>

<Maybe.>

Kira walked in a small circle and took a slow breath. *<Completing this mission is my first priority, but it does concern me that we keep getting deeper into this ship. We've already been in here longer than I anticipated, and at this point, I honestly don't know how we're going to get back out in time—assuming we do get the equipment in place.>*

Jasmine didn't reply.

<This is the part where you're supposed to tell me everything is going to be okay,> Kira prompted, but the AI was clearly distracted.

<Oh, I didn't expect that,> Jasmine said at last.

<I really can't handle any more vague statements right now.>

<I have made a significant discovery about how this ship operates and extrapolated that to an explanation for the Trols' behavior as a race,> the AI explained.

Kira stopped pacing. <Go on...>

<In the Guard's attempts to understand the structure, we have been approaching it like a ship. For that matter, we have been thinking about the Trols as individuals with their own motivations, as we observed with Nox and Reya.

<In reality, though, this ship operates like an organism, not a mechanical ship—except the nervous system is disaggregated in a way I have never encountered before. I had expected there to be one core that controlled everything, but instead there appears to be a node for each major function. I now believe that the Trol 'pits' are incubators for the specialized systems. It is where the beings learn to blend together into one voice.>

<Shite, so calling them a 'nest' wasn't far off... it's a nursery,> Kira realized.

<Yes, I believe that would be an apt analogy.>

Kira crossed her arms. <But what about all the evil shite going on? Possessing Kaen, Chancellor Hale, the plot with the Robus...>

<That's what I was trying to figure out. Those actions don't fit with the collective design of a craft such as this. I was quiet for so long because I was running through the scenarios of why that may be. This ship's design demands a cohesive community to

operate it, but none of the pieces on this ship are talking to each other. We have observed strong individualist tendencies at odds with the collective.>

Kira wanted to scream at the AI for taking so long to explain. <What did you figure out?!>

<This group has gone rogue.>

That was it? The big explanation?

Kira shook her head. <What in the stars are you talking about?>

<It explains everything,> Jasmine replied. <A group within the Trols decided they wanted individual expression. A scouting party set out to learn and grow—precisely what Nox explained to you. They settled upon Valta, a world rich in the valteron they needed to propagate. When Tarans settled in the Elvar Trinary, it was a chance to spread beyond Valta. They began growing new nurseries to increase their numbers, launching a plan that would maximize the cultivation of the negative emotional energy they needed to make them stronger.

<However, they weren't alone in their interest to break away from the rest of the collective. They needed to get a signal to their collaborators back home, wherever that may be, and relay that they had a foothold into the rest of the galaxy. This ship may have been waiting hundreds or thousands of years to receive that message. So, the Trols in Gaelon built the massive transmitter we observed. We had assumed it was pointed inward toward Empire space, but I believe we had it backwards all along.>

Kira allowed the words to sink in. <It's only been a month since then. If it was broadcasting into deep space, how the fok did the ship get here so quickly?>

<We have no understanding of the propulsion system on this craft. It is entirely possible that it has some form of jump

tech that works in a different way to ours. It did appear seemingly out of nowhere, after all—that is consistent with subspace travel.>

<Well, shite. Huh.> Kira uncrossed her arms and stared up at the rock node. <So, in theory, once we take out this ship, we'll be done with the rogue Trols.>

<Presumably. If there were others, I'd expect those carrier slots in the cylinders to be full. The fact that this ship is empty indicates that they pooled their resources and set out to grow their numbers.>

<Right, hence the plot with taking over the Elvar Trinary. But... who are the other Trols?>

<I can offer no insight into that,> the AI replied.

<I guess it doesn't matter.> Kira shook her head. <Back to the critical items now. Assuming this ship is controlled by a group of rogue Trols, and none of them want to play nice—which may be why the ship's parts aren't talking to each other—that doesn't help us access the systems we need to access.>

<No, it doesn't,> Jasmine agreed. <I probably shouldn't have even brought this up now. It's not relevant to our mission.>

<Actually, it's given me the beginning of an idea.>

<Please share, because I don't have a suggestion for how to proceed.>

<Were you able to identify what this node is responsible for?> Kira asked. <If it's not communications, then...?>

<Structural control.>

<Meaning?>

<I believe this node is what's controlling the internal movements of the corridors.>

Kira laughed. <Oh, shite, really? That makes it way easier! I was about to suggest some crazy convoluted thing with hacks,

tricks, and whatever other nonsense.>

   <Okay, so what do you have in mind?>

   Kira smiled. *<All we need to do is tell this node exactly where we want to go.>*

CHAPTER 18

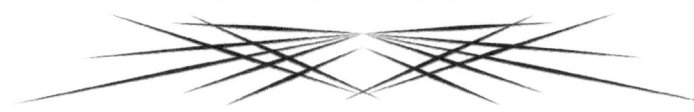

"STATUS!" KAEN ORDERED.

"No word from Kira or the *Raven*, sir," the comm tech reported.

"I have detected no friendly signal within the alien ship," Rianne added.

She should have been in touch by now. Kaen shifted in his seat.

Infiltrating any enemy compound always came with the risk that communications would be lost inside. Usually, there was some means to counter the interference. The device Kyle had designed should have allowed Kira to tap into the alien ship's own communications array, but clearly something had gone wrong.

"Can you reach her telepathically?" Kaen asked Jason.

The Agent shook his head. "I've been trying, but the entire planet-ship is clouded with some sort of telepathic interference. I can't pick her out from the din."

Kaen groaned inwardly. With the communications

blackout and no other sign, they had no way of knowing if Kira would be able to complete her mission, or even know if she was alive. Kaen only had his faith that she wouldn't give up.

Regardless of his concern for her safety, they were out of time. The Trol ship would be visible in the Elvar Trinary within five minutes. Even if Kira were to make her exit at that moment, an explosion wouldn't happen until it was well within visual range.

"Send the override order to the shield generators in the Elvar Trinary," he instructed.

"Sent," the comm tech confirmed.

Kaen slumped in his seat. "Now we wait."

— — —

A warning flashed across Ellen's computer monitor.

Is this it? She'd been waiting for the moment of truth—what, exactly, the Guard's 'visual disturbance' would be with their alleged 'test'. The warning about an offworld signal tapping into the control module for the shields indicated that she was about to find out.

She hit the comm on her desk. "Trisha, did you get the alert?"

"Yeah, the data packet is still downloading. It should be live in two minutes."

"I'll meet you in Ops Central."

She jogged down the hall past the bullpen of cubicles to the bank of windows on the far wall, which overlooked the courtyard between the Mysaran government building and MTech headquarters. More importantly for the present, it offered a clear view of the sky through the top of the translucent biodome.

It was twilight, and the stars were beginning to show alongside two of Mysar's three moons. The deep blue sky had a slight haziness to it from a nearby windstorm, but otherwise was perfectly clear.

"Anything yet?" Trisha asked, coming up behind her.

"No. I'm not even sure what to look for."

"Maybe it will be nothing."

Ellen shook her head. "I doubt that. The fact that they gave a warning at all means it will be significant. If anything, those kinds of announcements downplay the reality."

Trisha crossed her arms. "Well, we distributed our press release about the 'test'. I just sent an alert to the news networks that it was about to begin. It should be on every screen momentarily."

Ellen peered down at the massive reader board above the MTech lobby entrance. Sure enough, there was a red crawler along the bottom of the viewscreen stating that a planetary shield test was in progress.

Murmurs of surprise sounded around the room.

She returned her gaze upward in time to see an opaque spot in the upper atmosphere above the city, which was slowly growing. It spread across the shield like a pool of paint flowing around a sphere. Wherever it covered, the light dimmed only a small measure, but the stars and moons were completely obscured.

"I was expecting some flickering!" Trisha exclaimed. "This…"

"I know why the Guard is doing it, but I don't know how we explain this to the public." Ellen shook her head.

"Why block out the night sky?"

"Well, on the one hand, they're doing us a favor by hiding the planet-ship from view of the people on the surface. Dealing with the handful of people in the spaceport above the shield is way easier."

"That's true." Trisha nodded. "But you think there's another reason?"

"Yeah, the real reason. They've been evasive about how, exactly, they intend to take down that absurdly big ship. Whatever weapon they have that's capable of that level of destruction, they don't want anyone to know what it is—or that they even have it. If no one sees it, it's hearsay."

"I guess we'll need to keep our mouths shut, too."

Ellen released a long breath. "Sometimes it's a burden, having more information than anyone else and needing to keep it to yourself. Personally, though, I'd rather keep a secret and know the truth than blindly follow on the outside."

"I'm with you there."

"Ma'am?" a tech said from one of the nearby cubicles. "Daily News has someone on the line asking to do an interview about this shield test."

Ellen smiled at Trisha. "Why don't you take this one?"

"I don't know..."

"It should come from a local. If they interview me, it might make them more suspicious."

Trisha sighed and nodded. "All right."

"Come on, let's jot down some talking points."

— — —

Kira frowned at the code running through her mind. *<Okay, so maybe telling the node where we want it to take us wasn't as straightforward as I'd hoped.>*

Whenever she watched Kyle and Nia work on a hack, they'd made it look easy. As an AI, Jasmine had innate skill in computer-related endeavors, but the Trols' programming language was as alien as their lifeform.

<We might need to try something else,> Kira suggested.

<No, you're right. This is the best strategy. I know there's a way we can tell this ship to move this node to where we need to be, or at least how to open a pathway right to it.>

They'd already been working on it for fifteen minutes. The clock was ticking down too quickly.

<Jasmine—>

<Wait, I've got it!> the AI exclaimed. *<Watch this magic.>*

The ground trembled, and a hole appeared five meters to the left. Descending into the depth was a perfectly formed spiral staircase, made of the same stone-like material that was present throughout the ship.

Kira gaped at the creation. *<You're amazing! I'd ask you how you did it, but I don't think I want to know.>*

<Take the gift and go! The program is still running, and it will open a path for us back to the shuttle, too.>

<That's a long way up now.>

<But it won't be. I have programmed the bottom of the cylinder to lower to the level of the core. It should be a straight run for us, and then we can fly out.>

<That would have been such an easier way to get in!>

<Hindsight, and all that. We never could have hacked it remotely. They could override my commands at any time, though. We need to hurry. Kyle and Nia can keep it active for us once they get remote access.>

<Can you? Keep it open, I mean?>

<Not without an additional processor. Your mind is amazing, Kira, but it doesn't have the resources for an ongoing hack like that.>

<Understood. What about the device?> She looked down at

the box still resting on the ground by the column.

<*I'm using it to temporarily keep the doorway open. Leave it.*>

Without further delay, Kira raced down the stairs.

After the equivalent of twenty stories, her legs were burning, despite her augmentations. Rapid healing or not, she suspected she'd be feeling all the running around tomorrow.

She descended another fifteen stories before she finally spotted the bottom. To her right, she saw a surprisingly straight tunnel that faded into darkness.

<*That'll be our exit,*> Jasmine explained. <*Head left. We're almost there.*>

Kira ran in the indicated direction, her movements feeling odd over the flat ground, after spending so much time on the stairs.

<*How deep are we now?*>

<*Don't think about that. We have our exit plan,*> Jasmine replied.

The left path led through a corridor with a ceiling curving above her fifteen meters up, transitioning into rippled walls. The floor was the same spongy covering of interwoven fibers that she'd encountered in the depths of the ship, and it gave extra bounce to her step as she ran.

After half a kilometer, the broad passageway flared outward into a chamber that dwarfed the others.

<*This is the core,*> Jasmine stated as Kira entered.

A central column of rock rose in the center of the chamber, adorned by what looked like petals of a blooming flower, crafted from the same stone. It towered at least a kilometer high, but Kira couldn't get a clear reading on the top.

<*This node is connected to the rest of the ship,*> Jasmine explained. <*Communications, defenses—we can get it all from*

here.>

<So, we patch in, and then Kyle and Nia will keep it locked down while we escape?>

<That's the plan.>

<Okay, tell me where I hook this up.> Kira pulled the main module from her bag.

She jogged toward the central column, listening for any enemies that may be lurking in the shadows. In a space so large, anyone could be watching her without her knowledge.

The fibrous groundcover thickened closer to the column, and Kira was soon sinking in, up to the middle of her shins. Thanks to the field around her suit, the fibers moved from her path with every step. Without that, though, she feared it would be able to swallow her up in moments.

<Put it in physical contact with one of the data conduits. That will give a backup connection in case the wireless interface fails.>

<How do I use this tracer thing to find it?> Kira asked.

<I'll add a visual overlay for you. This might be a little... disorienting.>

Kira's vision distorted in a pixelated flash. When it cleared, there was an eerie purple glow to the environmental features around her. Some spots were bright, and others were almost black.

<What is this?>

<Electromagnetic field overlay. The brighter the spot, the more energy is running through it. You see that conduit in the central column?>

Kira nodded. It stood out from the others, both in brightness and thickness. <That's this node's primary connection with the rest of the ship, isn't it?>

<That's my best guess, anyway,> Jasmine said. <We'll know

right away if it works or not.>

Kira slogged through the moss-like fibers toward the part of the bright conduit that appeared to be closest to the surface. When she reached out her hand, it sank into the bed of flexible fibers and then touched stone underneath.

<Can you dim the visual overlay? I need to look at this,> she requested.

The purple faded from her vision.

Sure enough, the conduit she needed to access was deep within the column, without any discernable access point. *<Are you sure we need a physical connection?>*

<Without it, I fear the ship will be able to override the wireless signal much faster. It may buy us a minute or two, but seconds could make the difference.>

<All right, time to get creative.> Kira returned the module to her bag.

She stuck her hand into the mat of fibers covering the stone column, working them inward and tearing away the covering to expose the stone underneath.

<It needs to be in contact with the conduit inside.>

<I know,> Kira replied to the AI.

She pressed her fingertips into the rock. They sank in slightly, where the field around her suit made contact with the stone, breaking apart the bonds that held it together.

<Can you turn up the intensity?>

Jasmine smiled in her mind. *<Why didn't I think of that?>*

An electric spark shocked Kira's arm, but she blocked out the discomfort. Curling her fingers into a fist, she punched into the stone.

Her hand disappeared into the column, up to her wrist.

<This is super weird...>

<Don't go too deep!> Jasmine warned. *<We don't want to*

disrupt the conduit itself.>

The electromagnetic overlay returned to Kira's vision. She could see the outline of the shield around her hand and where her fist was in relation to the conduit. She'd need to go as deep as her elbow to reach it.

She worked her arm in until her fist was brushing the edge of the conduit. Then, she dragged it downward to create a vertical slit in the column wall large enough to slip the module inside.

While sliding her right arm up and down to keep the hole from closing, she readied the module in her left hand.

Kira quickly withdrew her right arm and then carefully slid the device into place, the pronged end pointed toward the conduit. The rock stayed clear of the field surrounding the device.

When the prongs were in contact with the conduit, Kira slid her arm out from the opening.

<That was a little more... intimate than I was expecting.>

<Yeah, I'm not going to take the bait and degrade into a conversation riddled with innuendo. I need to hack into this comm system.>

<Good plan,> Kira agreed.

Jasmine was silent for two minutes while she became acquainted with the network.

<And we have contact! Tapped into the communication system now. Pinging the Raven.*>*

A moment later, a chirp sounded in Kira's comm.

"*Raven*, can you hear me?" she asked.

"Kira! Thank the stars," Sandren replied. "It's been over two hours. What happened?"

"Ran into some moving passageways and mutant rock-dogs. The usual."

The major was silent. "Are… you okay?"

"Yes, sir. I'm at one of the inner nodes now."

"Wait, what?" Kyle said, jumping on the communication link. "You were only supposed to tap into one of the conduits running to the node."

"Yeah, well, that plan didn't work. It was a great idea, but this ship is all kinds of foked up."

"What do you mean?" the major asked, concern evident in his tone.

"The components aren't integrated in the way we had anticipated," Jasmine supplied. "I have come to believe that this group of Trols is a rogue faction."

"Meaning there are other Trols?" Sandren clarified.

"Possibly, sir. This is all speculation," Kira responded. "But this ship isn't built-out. It's like a bunch of disaggregated parts were thrown together by a group of people who don't want to work together."

"I'm not sure I follow, Captain…"

"I'll explain once I'm back, sir. The important part is that we needed to get to this central node in order to access the necessary parts. Jasmine has a wedge in the door for you."

"Yes! I see the access point," Kyle said.

"It's going to take some time to trace the defensive controls," Nia said, speaking up for the first time in the conversation.

"Good, because we'll need some time to get out of here," Kira said. "It'd be nice to have a chance to get back to you before the *Conquest* blows this thing."

"You might want to be careful about vocalizing those plans," Sandren cautioned.

"Pretty sure they picked up our intention when the *Conquest* attacked last time."

"We have your back. Get out of there, ma'am," Kyle said.

<Handoff is complete,> Jasmine reported in her mind. *<Let's see if our shuttle made it to where it's supposed to be.>*

"I'll see you soon," Kira told her teammates. She muted the comm.

<What do we do if it's not?> she asked Jasmine.

<We get to find out how fast you can climb.>

Kira ran toward the open passageway leading in the direction of the shuttle. She'd gone no more than four steps when a chorus of voices filled her mind.

"Where are you going, Kira? We're not finished with you yet."

CHAPTER 19

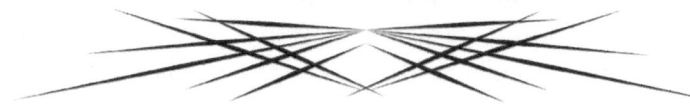

KIRA FROZE IN her tracks—not restrained by a physical force, but by a command in her mind.

<Shite! Jasmine, how are they doing this?>

Her heart pounded in her ears. They hadn't been able to overpower her—not since she faced off against Reya on Mysar, when the Trol was inside Chancellor Hale.

<I don't know. I can't sense it. I'm sorry, Kira, there's nothing I can do. You have to fight it.>

<Help me shift!>

<I'm trying, but there's something blocking it.>

Fok. Kira tugged against the invisible restraints binding her, but she couldn't trace where they were coming from. It was as though the air in the room had congealed around her.

Her mind raced as she thought about the possibilities— what might make this encounter different than the others.

<Jasmine, are there any foreign bodies inside me? Did that creature inject me with something when it bit me earlier?>

The AI was quiet—too quiet for Kira's liking.

<You found something, didn't you?>

<There is something, yes,> Jasmine replied. *<I didn't detect it before because it wasn't active.>*

<I'm guessing it is now.>

<It appears to be composed of valteron, only this nanotech is distributed throughout your nervous system.>

<You have to disable it.>

<I don't know if I can.>

<I'm frozen here!>

"You don't need to fight it, Kira," the chorus of voices said in her mind. They spoke together, but there were distinct tones layered in the statements, like they wanted to talk together but weren't well-rehearsed. *"You've run for so long, you've never even heard what we have to say."*

"Fine, then talk," she replied, with no genuine intention of hearing them out. The moment she had the upper hand, she would be out of there and on her ship, headed back to the *Conquest*, and then they'd blow these Trol fokers into oblivion once and for all.

The bonds holding her loosened ever so slightly, allowing her to place her foot, which had been left awkwardly in midair when she was frozen midstride, on the ground.

"You assume we are the enemy, but you know nothing of us."

"I don't know where you come from," Kira retorted, *"but around here, we have an ancient expression that states 'actions speak louder than words'. I know you communicate telepathically and all, but the same principle still applies. So, let's go over what you've done—that I know of. First, there was holding a bunch of people prisoner. Then there were the people whose bodies you stole for your own. And then there's the whole part about forcing genetic modifications on people. You can say*

you're not our enemy, but that's pretty antagonistic."

The chorus laughed. *"Is it wrong to enslave animals for slaughter and consume a lesser being? You do it all the time."*

"That's for food—for our survival."

"As you are to us."

<*Well, shite. They caught me in a logic loop I can't talk my way out of,*> she said to Jasmine.

<*Don't tell me what they're saying actually makes sense.*>

<*Without getting into an argument about the nature of sentience, they have essentially asserted that we are to them what cattle are to us.*>

<*You can't reason with a being whom perceives such a disparity between our stations in this universe,*> the AI said.

<*No, I can't. But hubris has a way of coming back to bite someone in the ass.*>

Kira returned her attention to the aliens. *"If Tarans and others like us are so inferior to you, then why bother talking to me?"*

"We left our physical forms long ago, but some of us have come to miss the pleasures of a corporeal existence," the chorus replied.

"Yeah, well, that doesn't give you an excuse to go take whatever body you see fit."

"We do not wish to take the form of those we have seen. They are imperfect and lack a sufficient connection to the innate universal energies. We wish to move at will."

"Does part of your being reside in subspace?"

"You would not understand the nature of an existence that isn't tied to one place or time."

"Above time?" Kira's heart leaped. *"Are you suggesting that you're fifth-dimensional beings?"*

The chorus laughed again. *"You Tarans and your simple concepts. All you must know is that we have been seeking a vessel to return us to our corporeal roots—one which we may inhabit for as long as we see fit, jumping between bodies and gaining power from their use."*

"You mean sending a soldier into war and gaining pleasure from its pain."

"Pain and anger... those have always been the greatest fuels. The others never agreed, but that is why they have remained weak."

"What others?" Kira asked.

She and Jasmine had discussed the possibility at length over the past month, speculating about other Trols who were drawn to the positive emotional spectrum for their fuel. Jasmine's discovery about the ship earlier in the day had supported that theory, but this was the first admission from a Trol that there might, indeed, be others with a counter point of view. It was a glimmer of hope that defeating this ship might offer a lasting chance at peace and not just another reprieve until a bigger assault.

The chorus chattered amongst itself for a moment—a cacophony Kira couldn't begin to decipher. It would seem there was some disagreement regarding the other Trols.

"The others have no ties to us," the chorus replied at last. *"They remain one, but we are many."*

"Yet you still speak as a 'we'," Kira pointed out, hoping to get some kind of rise out of them.

"And you speak of your nations as if all citizens are one, even though you emphasize individuality. Are we not afforded the same distinctions?"

"An interesting argument, given how flippantly you disregarded individual life when it came to inhabiting Kaen and

Hale."

"*Necessary pawns to further our ends.*"

"*Yeah, well, maybe we aren't as simple as you think we are. You insist on your superiority and the worth of your life over ours, but we continue to best you.*"

The chorus closed around her like a dark cloud. "*When you destroyed our world in Gaelon, we learned from you. You can't stop us now.*"

Kira ignored them. <*Is the comm link still up?*> she asked Jasmine.

<*Yes, the device is functioning perfectly.*>

<*I was hoping you'd say that.*>

She smiled at the Trols inside her mind. "*Yeah, see, you talk a big game, and yet you haven't been able to stop us. Are you going to deny that I stuck my hand right through your walls and planted that device? You can make all the threats you want, but the fact remains that you can't remove that module, or you would have done it already. For all your talk of 'we' and your collective, you're so intent on destruction that you've forgotten how to work together. And that's where we have you beat. We are driven by bonds of love and duty—and those will always be stronger than anger and hate.*"

"*We have you, Kira. If* you *could have escaped, you would have done so by now.*"

"*See, that's where you're wrong.*" She smirked. "*I've been stalling.*"

In the background, Kira had been keeping part of her mind focused on the comm link to the *Raven* while giving her mini-speech. The link grounded her, offering a tangible connection to her friends—her work family—for whom she'd do anything. That bond had always been a force to use against the Trols, and it was no different now.

When transforming in the past, she had often used anger as her fuel. This time, she was building her reserves on the positive spectrum. She was going to beat the Trols, and it would be on her terms.

With a surge of energy, she snapped the invisible bonds holding her, using the momentum to spur a transformation into her Robus state.

The Trols were caught off-guard, the chorus crying out in her mind with surprise and anger.

"You can't hold me," she told them. *"You may be many, but the strength of individuals working together for good will* always *be more powerful than those seeking destruction."*

Her body broadened into the powerful fighting beast that had always been in her heart, even when she didn't have the physical form to match. Now she was complete, and she was going to make sure this bad batch of Trols wouldn't be able to harm anyone again.

— — —

"We have a connection!" exclaimed the *Conquest*'s comm tech.

Kaen jumped up from his seat in Central Command.

"Patch me through to the *Raven*."

Major Sandren appeared onscreen, standing to the side of Kyle and Nia, who were seated at workstations in the *Raven*'s hangar.

"What's your status, Major?" Kaen asked.

"We just made contact with Kira. I have good news and bad," he replied. "She was able to install the device, and my team has successfully infiltrated the Trol vessel's systems. However, we haven't yet gained access to the defensive systems that previously prevented the disruptor from performing."

Kaen nodded. "We figured this wouldn't be instantaneous. You just need more time?"

"Correct, sir. Jasmine gave us a big head start, and we're close."

"I don't see what's bad about any of that."

"It's not about the hack, sir. Kira needed to venture deeper into the ship than we'd anticipated. She's presently more than twenty-three kilometers beneath the surface."

Kaen's heart sank. "Is she on her way out?"

"We... think so."

"Major?"

Sandren shook his head. "We lost verbal contact with her shortly after we established the connection with the ship's system. The comm link is open but muted."

"Then let's find her! If you're patched into the ship's systems, then surely you can locate her."

"It's taking all of our computer resources and know-how to keep the backdoor open. Jasmine added in some extra measures that we hadn't accounted for."

Kaen's brow knitted. "Like what?"

"She seems to have reprogrammed the internal layout of the ship."

"How is that possible?"

"We'll need to wait for them to get back here to explain, sir. But the point is, the ship has a mind of its own, and it's rather angry about what we're doing to it."

"Sir!" Rianne interrupted. "The alien vessel increased velocity."

"Match its speed," Kaen said.

Next to him, Jason tensed. "Estimated time to arrival in the Elvar system decreased by seven hours at our new speed."

Shite, if we get any closer than six hours, the debris field will be too close to the system to hide. "She'll need to be out in the next hour," he replied.

"Hopefully it will be less than that, sir," Sandren said, having overhead the conversation. "I don't think Kyle and Nia will be able to hold off the counter-defenses for more than another twenty minutes, even with CACI's assistance."

"Don't underestimate us, sir," Kyle said with a slight smile from the workstation behind him. "We could do this all day."

"You're being a showy ass," Nia countered with bite in her tone, eyes narrowed. "We're barely holding it together. Be honest."

"Okay, yeah, things could be better," Kyle admitted.

"Sir, we're to the final security block," Nia continued. "Once we break through this, the ship's defenses will come down. After we execute, we'll have five minutes tops."

"Can you hold here?" Kaen asked.

Kyle and Nia exchanged glances. "For a little while, but we can't say for how long," he replied.

Guard soldiers are prepared to die for the greater good, Kaen reminded himself.

Kira entered that ship knowing full well she might not make it out again. The way of the soldier. Honor. Courage. Commitment. The ideals were the foundation of the Guard. But it wasn't just her in there; Jasmine was along for the ride. Though created through alternate means, hers was a sentient life, all the same.

Two lives in exchange for a system.

The math was easy, but Kaen wouldn't throw away two soldiers' lives while there was still a chance to save everyone.

"How do you want to proceed?" Jason asked.

Stars! I can't fire on Kira not until it's our last resort

He switched back to the comm link with the *Raven*. "Continue to hold."

"Yes, sir," Sandren confirmed. "The Trols are putting up a bomaxed good fight, but we have the upper hand for now."

"And there's no way to identify Kira's position?"

"Not without putting our other efforts in jeopardy. We're waiting for acknowledgement that she's at the shuttle."

Shite, where is she? Kaen nodded. "Alert me as soon as she's en route, or if the Trols are at risk of regaining control of the defensive systems. We'll give her every moment we can spare."

CHAPTER 20

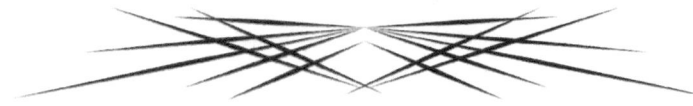

TELEPATHIC BONDS TRIED to pin Kira, but she slashed them back with a mental scythe. *"I'm not some lab specimen for you to possess!"*

"You are so close to what we need to become something more. With a form such as yours, and the superior intellect of our collective, we can dominate. We can make you one of us."

"I have no interest in joining your freaky cult!" she spat back as she ran. She morphed between her standard and Robus forms, ever-changing to prevent them from getting hold of her again.

"But don't you want to be part of something more? We can see into your mind—your heart. You are able to connect with other minds in a way that no one else of your kind can. You've always been alone, despite the bonds you've convinced yourself are enough. But we see it—we sense how you want to be part of something bigger than yourself."

"Don't you get it?" She scoffed in her mind. *"I am part of something bigger than myself. The Guard, the friends and family*

I have, the love of my partner—having those things does *make me more than what I am on my own. I don't need to kill and dominate others to achieve that."*

"You're so restricted! They are weaker than you. We made you something more, and yet you continue to answer to them."

"They're my friends. I continue to work with them because I care about them and the rest of the people in the Taran Empire. Personal sacrifice is what allows our people to prosper as a community."

She reached out her mind toward the Trols, probing to see what fueled them. The hate, the anger, the need to possess—it had to have come from somewhere.

The emptiness swirled in the ethereal space that existed between her mind and the collective consciousness of the ship. Looking at it cohesively, she could sense the disparate parts that Jasmine had picked up on in her digital analysis. The hundreds of Trol nests were striving for the same thing; ironically, that goal was to separate.

Kira tried to understand the underlying motivation. Her quest for inner truth was what had made her so effective at her job in the past, looking into people's minds to identify what drove them. Appeal to that inner desire, and the person was hers to command.

As she looked into the collective mind of the Trols, though, it was strangely empty. The thirst for pain that fueled them permeated every thought, but beyond that… there was a void.

To her surprise, her heart softened.

This thirst for pain wasn't driven by a fundamental, biological need; it was a reflection of what they already felt—isolation, loneliness. They sought to prolong that state of being because they no longer remembered another way to live.

"How did you get to be so bitter?" she asked them. *"Why do*

you seek out pain while others of your kind thrive on love?"

"*There* is *no other way!*" the chorus screamed.

Kira understood now. She had seen their inner self. This group was angry and bitter at the universe—essentially, immature teenagers acting out at the worlds. They were dissatisfied with their own existence, having not yet come into their own, and so they sought to make others suffer, and be a part of their own perceived suffering.

She felt sorry for them, to have stooped to that level. Such an ancient, powerful race could have been so much more, but hubris had been their undoing. Power, ambition… though their intentions came from a place of self-improvement, they were blinded by a singular focus on dominance.

To thrive, one needed to understand the larger context of their actions.

Examining the Trols made Kira appreciate that much more what the Taran Empire had done. To bring together so many different people who could have been enemies was one of the greatest accomplishments in the galaxy, across all time. It was a foundation from which they could grow toward a future with greater equity and justice.

"*Are you sure you won't reconsider?*" she asked them. "*This is your last chance to stand down.*"

"*If you won't join us, then you will die with the rest!*"

<*Well, that's a pretty clear answer,*> she said to Jasmine.

<*Negotiations didn't go well?*>

<*You can't reason with people who refuse to acknowledge there's another side. We've done everything we can. They chose this for themselves.*>

Kira never took death lightly, but she readily acknowledged it was a part of war. And right now, it was her duty to stop the war with the Trols before it claimed more innocent lives.

She broke the telepathic connection with the Trol collective. Driven by her desire to return to her loved ones, she sprinted toward the exit.

As Jasmine had promised, the corridor was a straight shot. The question was if the shuttle would be waiting for her at the end.

<I have the shuttle's homing signal!> Jasmine announced.

<Stars, that's a relief!>

<One problem, though. The planet-ship only restructured to bring the shuttle down to a level even with the top of the main chamber, not the bottom deck.>

Kira's heart skipped a beat. *<That's almost a kilometer up! Maybe more.>*

<I'm trying to work out a path to get there. Kyle and Nia are in the system, so I have access to an accurate real-time layout.>

<Can you have them move the pieces around to get the shuttle to this level?>

<There aren't sufficient computing resources—we're already at the bandwidth capacity of the backdoor into the network. We'll need to bootstrap our escape,> Jasmine said.

<We better get some sort of medal for this.>

The map in Kira's mind updated with a blue line tracing through a series of corridors on a zig-zagging incline, with one notable exception.

<Uh, Jasmine, that's a fifty-meter-tall vertical shaft.>

<Yes.>

<How am I—>

<You have claws, remember?> Jasmine interrupted. *<You punched straight into the stone before, and you can do it again.>*

Considering that she didn't have an alternative idea, Kira followed the new course.

She retraced her steps down the broad passageway, and then took a sharp right down a narrower passage into the chamber with the vertical shaft in the middle. The area beneath the shaft was covered with an especially thick patch of the spongy fibers.

<*This ship design doesn't make any sense.*>

<*I believe these chutes were used by the biological guards we encountered earlier.*>

Kira frowned. <*Think there are more of them?*>

<*Almost certainly. Whether or not we will cross paths, I don't know.*>

Until they were right in front of her, there was no point in worrying about what may or may not be around the next bend.

She looked up at the shaft, four meters above her. <*That's a bomaxed big leap.*>

<*You can make it with a running start. You'll need to dig your claws in and haul yourself up. I ran the models based on the baseline I established in training, and you can do this.*>

Kira drew a deep breath. <*Okay, here it goes.*>

She took six rapid strides toward the shaft, pushing off with her legs on the final step. She launched into the air toward the opening.

The stone was barely within her grasp. She extended her arm and thrust her claws into the stone. As she made contact, her momentum carried her past her mark, causing her claws to slip.

She swung her other arm upward and plunged it into the stone to steady herself. However, the field around her slowly began to disintegrate the stone, and she slid downward.

<*You need to adjust the intensity!*> she shouted to Jasmine in her mind.

<*I'm trying...*>

Only four centimeters remained between Kira's claws and the bottom of the shaft.

Her downward slide slowed, but didn't stop completely.

<You need to adjust the field around each hand as I move.> Kira withdrew her right claws and swung herself upward to grab above her head. When her claws were locked into place, she repeated the motion with her left. After two more laborious swings, she was finally able to secure her feet on the stone ripples underneath her.

She looked down. *<Psh, easy.>*

<Climb!> Jasmine shouted.

Looking upward, Kira realized how far fifty meters was. *<I suddenly miss those stairs from earlier.>*

<Less lamenting, more vertical motion. Kyle and Nia won't be able to hold off the defenses for much longer.>

Kira raced up the vertical rock face, using her claws and feet to propel her upward. Once she got in the rhythm, she accelerated into super-speed.

She rocketed out of the top and into the center of a chamber. Three passageways fanned out in opposite directions. The map flashed in her mind, pointing her up a ramp to the right.

Kira charged toward the opening, but her feet were knocked out from underneath her midstride.

When she caught herself with her hands, she looked back to see a creature like the ones she'd encountered on her way in. It rounded on her, fangs bared.

<Shite, where did that come from?>

<Apparently, they've been waiting for us.>

<I've had enough of this shite!> Kira slashed at the beast, raking her claws across its side.

The creature yelped and recoiled, its hindquarters only a

step from the shaft's lip.

Kira kicked it in its wounded side, knocking it through the opening. *<That's how it's done!>*

<Kira… look behind you.>

Two dozen beasts crouched in the shadows, ready to pounce. The four luminescent eyes above each of their powerful jaws were filled with bloodlust. One daring creature slinked forward, snarling at Kira.

"If you won't join us in life, then your death will bring us pleasure," the chorus of Trol voices whispered at the edge of her consciousness.

<Nope.>

Kira sprinted for the passageway leading to the shuttle. She could hear the pack of creatures loping behind her, but she kept her attention ahead.

<You can outpace them, but we need time to get inside the shuttle,> Jasmine warned.

Kira already felt like she was running as fast as she could, but she pushed even harder. The world around her changed— almost like it was skipping forward. Features in the passageway that had seemed far away were suddenly next to her.

Kira didn't know what was happening, but she didn't care. All that she knew was she had to put distance between her and her attackers, and her shuttle was right up ahead.

The Trols still beckoned at the edge of her mind, asking her to stay. The tone of their most recent pleas had soured, changing to a request for her to stay so that they could 'dissect' her and 'revel in her suffering'.

It wasn't a good sales message.

She burst into an open chamber, the stone walls extending upward further than she could see. At the center of the open space was her shuttle, seemingly undamaged. It still rested on the fibrous material it had landed on, but everything else was different.

On her final approach to the craft, Kira peered upward, and that's when she noticed faint pinpricks of light.

<Well done sinking the ground around the shuttle,> she said to Jasmine.

<When you can reprogram the insides of a ship, sometimes the simplest solutions are the best.>

Kira raced into the back hatch of the shuttle and closed the door. She wasn't sure how far behind her those creatures might be, and she didn't want to find out.

<They'll be here in thirty seconds,> Jasmine supplied as she powered up the shuttle and tapped into the navigation controls. *<We're clear of them, but Kyle and Nia are on their last legs. The Trols will regain control within four minutes, and we'll lose the window to launch the disruptor cannon attack.>*

<Cutting it awfully close.>

<Those little delays added up,> Jasmine said as the shuttle shot upward toward open space. *<I'll get us to the* Raven *as fast as I can.>*

Millions of voices called out to Kira as the shuttle zoomed through the cylinder and up into open space. She ignored them, letting out a little laugh. As she relaxed, she returned to her standard form. *<That was the craziest thing I've ever done.>*

<I'll celebrate when we're out of blast range.>

Kira noticed the countdown clock in the corner of the shuttle's front viewport. The arrival time to the *Raven* and the opportunity window for the assault on the Trol ship were only seconds apart.

<We'll make it. A whole four seconds to spare!>

Jasmine didn't reply.

The *Raven* came into view up ahead, and few things had

ever been a more welcome sight in Kira's life. However, her joy was cut short when she saw the telltale signs of the engines igniting.

<Fok! They're about to leave without us.>

<Bay door is still open. I'm taking us in!>

Kira secured her harness. She held her breath and gripped the armrest. *We have to make it back. We're so close now...*

She had been willing to give her life for the mission when it was about venturing into the unknown, but now that she was so close to success and safety, she wanted nothing more than to be back with her team... and to see Leon again.

The *Raven* went from a distant speck to taking up the shuttle's viewport in an instant. They were coming in way too fast to dock.

<Oh, shite, we're not going to make it...> Kira's heart dropped.

Then the *Raven* rolled to the side and began accelerating away from the shuttle, matching its trajectory.

<Wait, they're going to line up with us so we can get on board!> she realized.

<Only a fighter pilot like Rodrick would think of that.>

Kira remained silent while Jasmine made the necessary adjustments to pull off what by all accounts should be an impossible maneuver. The remaining distance between the two craft closed quickly, and the shuttle came into alignment with the bay entrance. She half-closed one eye and braced.

A bang, followed by the squeal of grinding metal, assaulted Kira's senses. She was knocked sideways and would've been sent tumbling from her chair, were it not for her harness holding her in place.

The shuttle came to rest in an emergency net.

Kira breathed a sigh of relief. Looking out the front

viewport, she saw her team's temporary workspace a mere four meters away. Without the emergency net, her teammates would have been a splat on the bay wall—and her, too, for that matter.

<Jasmine, I never want to do that again.>

— — —

"Shuttle just reached the *Raven!*" Rianne announced.

Kaen straightened in his chair. *Only three minutes and twenty-seven seconds to go. Kyle and Nia need to hold on.*

"Maintain your position," he ordered. "Shields in the Elvar Trinary are still tinted?"

"Yes, sir," the comm tech acknowledged.

"Charging the weapon now," Jason said. He gripped the handholds on the podium in front of his seat.

An electrical hum filled the air as the ship built up the charge—this time, building toward the maximum Jason could safely handle.

Kaen watched the progress of the *Raven* onscreen. Despite its actual speed, it appeared to be lazily approaching the *Conquest* across the vast span between them.

He couldn't believe Sandren had authorized the reckless shuttle retrieval. As much as Kaen wanted to see Kira home safely, having the shuttle come in hot like that had put the entire mission at risk at the last second. If any of the calculations had been off, the shuttle could have easily careened into Kyle and Nia's workstations, and that would have been the end of their security bypass.

They *had* made it, though, and they were about to blast the Trol bastards out of existence.

"Thirty seconds to clearance from blast range!" Rianne

updated.

Almost there...

The final seconds ticked down onscreen. Kaen took a deep breath right before it reached zero.

"Fire!"

Jason released the energy charge.

The blast shot across open space to the Trol ship. The energy beam collided with the vessel, lancing through it with a spectacular plume of blue light. Secondary explosions rippled through the ship as it collapsed slightly, and then it began folding inward on itself. A bright flash in the center of the ship whited out the screen at the front of the bridge.

When it cleared, fragments from the Trol ship were hurtling outward, and the energy orb at the center of the ship swelled to encompass them. As the orb slowly contracted, no sign of the vessel remained.

Jason smiled, though he looked wiped out. "That's more like it."

— — —

Kira collapsed to the floor of the *Raven*'s bay as she stepped out of the shuttle, gripping her head.

Millions of minds screamed in agony. Somehow, she was still linked with them.

<*What's wrong?*> Jasmine asked frantically.

<*So... many...*> Kira could barely form the words in her mind.

When Gaelon had been destroyed, she had felt the Trols' pain in their final moments. But that was only one nest; this Trol ship had hundreds. Each of the millions of minds within the collective consciousness cried out in one last bid for life.

It sucked Kira in. Her invisible ties to them bound her mind to theirs, and as they faded, she found herself on the edge of an abyss staring into nothingness.

She tried to shift again, to break her hold, but she couldn't feel her body.

<*Jasmine!*> She wasn't sure if the call escaped her private mind.

The darkness closed in around her.

<*Kira!*> The AI was there, somewhere in the distance.

Kira tried to reach out to her, only she had no bearings. She was falling inside her own mind.

Then a new presence emerged.

The Trols' voices of hate and pain were gone, replaced by a distant chorus that drew her back toward her physical self.

Her eyes shot open, and she picked herself up off the ground.

<*Kira, are you all right?*> Jasmine asked.

<*Yeah, I'm fine now.*>

Ari and Sandren ran toward her, as Kyle and Nia rose from their workstations, their faces drawn with concern.

"What happened?" Sandren asked, offering to help her the rest of the way to her feet.

"I need to decontaminate before anyone touches me," she told him, standing upright on her own. "I think the Trols had some sort of hold on me up until the end. They're gone now."

He nodded. "The ship has been destroyed. It's over."

Kira breathed a sigh of relief. "Thank the stars!"

"It was foking spectacular!" Kyle grinned.

On the viewscreen set up behind the work area, a video of the sphere's explosion was replaying on a loop. Kira watched the beam slice through it and then the secondary explosion vaporize the entire structure. She had to admit, it was a sight to behold.

Nia looked her over. "You look like you've been through a slaughter. Is that blood all over you?"

"There were some... obstacles," she replied. "I spoke with the Trols briefly, when I was in the core. This was a rogue group. The ship had the last of the Trols who held those ideals."

Sandren released a long breath. "This is going to be an interesting debrief."

"That's for sure." Kira shook her head. "If you don't mind, I'll get in the decontamination booth now."

The major looked her over. "It would be inhumane to stand in your way."

"Hugs after you're not covered in... that," Kyle said, tracing his finger through the air from Kira's head to feet and back.

"Rock-dog blood. Don't you think it goes well with my hair?" Kira smirked. She had yet to see her own reflection, but she could only imagine the horror show.

"We'll see you soon. Well done," Sandren told her.

Kira jogged across the hangar to the decontamination stall. As she started to strip down, a bright chorus of voices suddenly spoke in her mind.

"*Thank you. Now we are free.*"

She jumped with surprise. "*Are you the others?*" Her heart pounded in her ears, but the fear only lasted a moment.

A warm glow filled Kira as the distant alien presence embraced her. She had no idea where they were in space, but in that moment, they were connected across the light years.

Joy washed over her—an elation so complete that the world around her melted away. She basked in the tranquil light surrounding her mind.

"*Who are you?*" she asked them.

"*We are life. Love, compassion, hate, greed—we understand the spectrum of experience. Some of us, unfortunately, fell to the darkness that lives within us all. But now, thanks to you, they are free of their burdens, and we may build anew.*"

"*We didn't know if there were others. I'm sorry we destroyed this ship and the world in Gaelon. I—*"

A sense of serenity filled Kira's mind. "*We understand what you did was necessary. You tried to stop them through other means first. Not everyone would have been so compassionate when faced with such a challenge.*"

"*I wish it hadn't come to that.*"

"*The cruelty that was in them is not our way. It needed to be stopped before it spread.*"

Kira nodded. "*I'd hoped there were others of your kind with different motivations. There's so much we want to learn from you! Your technology, everything you know—*"

"*You are still a young race,*" the chorus interrupted. "*It is not yet time for us to share all that we can offer, but we'll be watching you from afar. We see what your Empire has done for this galaxy, and we know its inhabitants are in good hands—especially yours.*"

The peaceful glow began to retreat from her mind, and Kira braced for the inevitable internal void when it left her. However, even as she sensed the presence loosening its connection to her, the feeling of fulfillment didn't diminish.

"*A parting gift,*" the voices said. "*Keep protecting those in need.*"

As quickly as they had arrived, the alien minds vanished.

"Wow," Kira murmured aloud.

<*Something unusual just happened,*> Jasmine said. <*New information appeared. It's like you have a new memory, except there's no record of it ever happening.*>

<What is it?>

<I believe it's instructions for how to regulate your hybrid nanites.>

Kira's heart leaped. <So, I could keep my new abilities, and you could make it so transformations won't hurt? I won't lose control?>

<I don't want to make promises, but my preliminary review suggests that is the case, yes,> the AI confirmed.

<Wow. Having full control of my abilities, what will I be able to do?>

Jasmine smiled in her mind. <It will be an adventure.>

CHAPTER 21

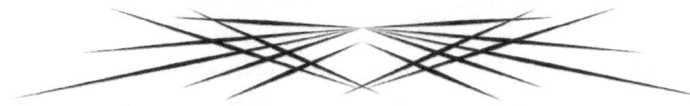

AS KIRA EXITED the docking concourse at Orion Station, a group of two dozen soldiers cheered and clapped.

<Uh, what?> None of the people looked familiar to her.

<The video of the ship's destruction was shared within the Guard. Your team was cited as carrying out the op that made it possible,> Jasmine explained.

<No one ever gathers like this.>

<The circumstances were different.>

The AI did have a point. Most missions took place almost exclusively in the field, with little support from base. In this conflict with the Trols, however, the fight had come inside the facility's walls. Though the battle itself was fought in a remote location, the victory rang as a shared triumph—the vanquishing of a foe that had impacted the lives of everyone in that division of the Guard in some way.

"Man, I could get used to this hero's welcome all the time," Ari said with a grin.

Kira smiled back. "Don't let it go to your head."

"Too late," Kyle ribbed. "Pretty sure he's already updated the bio on his main Net video account with 'galactic savior' as his official job title."

She scrunched up her nose. "Wasn't that on there already?"

Nia laughed. "Oh, Kira, you should know by now that Ari's ego knows no bounds."

"Formal debrief will be in thirty minutes. See you then," Sandren said as he passed by Kira and her team.

"Yes, sir," she acknowledged.

They took a couple of moments to thank the soldiers who'd come to greet them, and then headed toward their quarters to drop off their travel items before the meeting.

Kira was surprised Leon hadn't been waiting for her at the concourse, but she found him standing outside her quarters in his usual fashion. "There you are."

"Kira!" He ran to her, arms outstretched. He held her close. "I was so worried," he murmured into her hair.

"Being entombed in an alien death-planet-ship-thing wasn't high on my list of preferred ways to die."

Leon pulled back enough to look her in the eyes. "Are you okay?"

"Better than okay—especially now that I'm back home." She kissed him deeply, happy that he'd staged the reunion in a more private location.

Kira unlocked her door and showed him inside. "Is it true that word is getting around the Guard about what happened?"

"Not *around*-around, but a fair number of people know. I think a few people started talking about it before it was made clear that it's classified information."

"Doesn't surprise me."

Leon sat down on the edge of her bed. "What happened after the ship was blown up? Your message was really cryptic."

She joined him on the bed. "There are more of the Trols—or whatever they're actually called. The others aren't like the ones we met, though. They're good, and kind, and they see what we're doing in this galaxy and wish us the best."

"Advanced, then?"

"*So* advanced. Between us, I don't think we have a proper frame of reference yet to understand a lifeform like theirs."

"After everything I've seen, that doesn't surprise me."

She took his hand. "But it's over. The bad ones are gone."

Leon cupped his free hand on the side of Kira's face, and gave her a slow kiss. "What now?"

"First up, I have a debrief in twelve minutes."

He dropped his hands to his sides. "Of course you do."

"But after that, I honestly don't know. More missions and… whatever, I guess?" She paused. "Also, I sorta got offered a position with the TSS."

"The TSS?" Leon came to attention. "That would be a change."

"Yeah, I haven't decided how I feel about it yet. I think it was an open-ended offer."

"Then you have plenty of time to decide."

<Tell him about the information you got from the other Trols!> Jasmine prompted.

"Oh, and I have something science-y for you to work on," Kira continued. "I, uh, sort of 'communed' with the good counterparts of the Trols, and they passed some information on to me. Jasmine thinks it's a fix to my nanite problems."

"That's… very interesting."

"Yeah, so you should probably check that out."

He nodded. "I'd definitely like to take a look."

"Okay, how about I swing by the lab after the debrief?"

"Sounds good."

They parted ways with another kiss, and then Kira headed to the designated conference room.

She settled into her place at the table, across from Colonel Kaen and Major Sandren, with the three members of her team to her right.

"To state the obvious, all of you have done amazing work over the past several days," Kaen began. "You have demonstrated time and again how dedicated you are to your positions. You truly rose to the occasion, and you have the Guard's sincere gratitude."

"Of course, sir. Just doing our jobs," Kira replied, and her team murmured their agreement.

The colonel nodded. "Well, let's go over exactly what happened."

The team members each recounted their version of the events. Kira was surprised to hear how close her team had come to losing control while stalling for time as she made her way back to the *Raven*. By the time they were finished, she was convinced that anyone else would have left her to die. She owed them her life many times over.

Kaen took it in silently, nodding and making occasional notes in shorthand on the touch-surface tabletop. When every member of the team had completed their report, he smiled.

"These reports have confirmed my impressions of the events." He looked to the three soldiers on Kira's team. "Effective immediately, you're all promoted to the rank of corporal."

The three soldiers exchanged glances.

"Thank you, sir," Kyle said, "but doesn't that mean we're supposed to be squad leaders or something?"

"Rank is based on the needs of the Guard and the leadership positions we fill. Because of your work in special operations, none of you was afforded the opportunity to lead a squad. We know you could, and much more. It's time that was corrected." Kaen smiled. "Keep up this level of performance, and you'll find yourselves sergeants soon."

Kira beamed at her team. "Congratulations, Corporals."

They wouldn't say it out loud, but Kira could tell at least one of them was thinking something along the lines of 'about bomaxed time'.

"As for you, Kira," Kaen continued, "it's about time you were promoted to major."

Her heart skipped a beat. "Thank you, sir."

<Congratulations, Kira! Very well deserved,> Jasmine said in her mind.

Sandren smiled. "How many times do you have to prove your courage, commitment, and can-do attitude before you get something for your continued sacrifices?"

"I will fulfill my duty to the best of my ability."

"To that end, we'll need to reevaluate the best use of all of your skills moving forward. We'll figure out your assignments in the coming days," Kaen continued.

<Are they going to break us up?> Kira asked Jasmine.

<I don't know any more than you. There's always Jason's offer to join the TSS, if you don't like how things shake out in the Guard.>

<I was thinking the same thing.> Kira nodded to the colonel. "Yes, sir, we'll be standing by."

"Now, go celebrate. You've earned it," Kaen said with a smile. "I heard there's going to be cake."

— — —

Ellen settled into the chair across from President Joris'

desk. After more than a month away from Elusia, it was strange to be back in the place that had not long before been her home away from home.

"Quite an exciting month!" Joris said, smiling behind his steepled fingers.

"Drama I am very happy to now have behind me." Ellen sank into her chair.

"Has Trisha called you in a panic yet?" He smirked.

"Only twice, but I was able to talk her down both times."

"Good. I know you wouldn't have recommended her for the Mysaran governorship if she couldn't handle the position."

Ellen nodded. "There's no one else I'd feel more confident having in her role, especially with Fiona as her second-in-command. She's dedicated and sharp."

"I agree, that's a winning combination. Plus, she supports unity within the Elvar Trinary."

"Another benefit, for sure."

Joris tapped his fingertips together. "There is someone who's proven less than supportive on that front."

Ellen tilted her head quizzically.

"Mitchell Korwen."

"Right…" She let out a long breath, thinking back to her conversation with the mayor of Tribeca. It was unfortunate that she'd needed to resort to threats, but at least the matter had been resolved in time.

"As we move forward with unification," Joris continued, "having someone more agreeable would expedite matters considerably."

"Yes. Who do you have in mind?"

"You, actually."

Ellen laughed. "Yeah, right."

"Can you give me a good reason why not? We have always

emphasized the need for local representation in the political arguments we've made with these recent events. You're a Valtan native, and you've lived on all three worlds in this system. I can think of no better person to serve as a representative of Valtan interests while understanding the larger context of the political landscape."

She worked her mouth. "I'm not sure what to say…"

"You can start by accepting the role. Play bashful if you like, but I know you want this. In all your changes of allegiance, your commitment to Valta has never wavered."

"I don't know how you'll get the other representatives on the world to go along with it."

Joris smiled. "Let's just say I've already made a few calls to vet the idea, and I don't think there will be any issues."

Ellen thought for a moment. "Sir, I would be honored."

"Excellent."

"Then there's also the matter of transitioning you to president of this system, once Valta and Mysar are officially brought into the Empire."

"Formalities. And maybe someone else will want to run for that position. I'm happy I was able to get us this far, no matter what the future holds."

She took a deep, satisfied breath. "A united system, finally."

"We have a bright future together."

— — —

Kira drummed her fingers on her crossed arms. Leon and Jack had been absorbed in their computers for the past five minutes.

"What do you—?" she started to ask, but Jack suddenly pushed back from his station.

"This is everything we were missing before," he stated. "All the biological interactions with the tech, the control mechanisms, it's all here."

"What does that mean for me?" Kira asked.

"It means my initial assessment was correct," Jasmine replied over the lab's comms. "With this guide, I'll be able to control your transformations. The application requires an AI, so it's unlikely that use of the tech will become widespread. However, this means you'll be able to maximize your abilities—should you choose to do so."

"Being able to safely use super-speed? No complaints," Kira said.

"You've really embraced the new abilities," Leon commented.

"I know it's strange." Kira shrugged. "I hated that Monica forced these changes on me, but now that I've gotten used to the idea of the nanotech, the abilities *are* kind of awesome."

Jack grinned. "Fok yeah! You're on the road to total badassery."

"There is a downside to embracing the change, though." Kira slumped in her chair. "What'll happen to my team?"

"They'll be a whole lot safer," Leon replied.

"Yes, and that part's great. But with their promotions, and now me having control of these new abilities and my own promotion, I'm concerned that the higher-ups are going to separate us."

"A fascinating conundrum." Jack rose from his station. "And I'm sure you two will have a riveting discussion about it, but I'm gonna go ogle this data. I know how Leon hates it when I dissect your weird tech in his presence."

"Kira has expressed displeasure when I do that, as well," Jasmine chimed in over the comm.

"Shocking that talking about me like a science experiment doesn't give me the warm fuzzies," Kira muttered.

"Knock yourself out, Jack," Leon said to his coworker as he departed the lab.

"See ya." Jack waved goodbye and then closed the door behind him.

Kira rolled her eyes and sighed.

"At least he's useful." Leon shrugged. "Now, I believe we're at the part where I'm supposed to offer some insightful words of wisdom about life transitions and how friendships transcend current work assignments."

She smiled. "Yeah, that sounds about right."

"I thought so." Leon crossed his arms and frowned. "Bomax, I've got nothing."

Kira raised an eyebrow. "Seriously?"

He grinned. "Nah, I'm just messing with you." He extended his arms toward her.

She took his hands, and he drew her in for a kiss.

"Look," he said when they parted, "I know change can be scary and sad and all those other feelings we try to avoid, but sometimes that's exactly what we need in order to grow and really come into our own. Whether your team structure changes, or you have different assignments, or even if you do decide to join the TSS instead, it's a chance for you to try something new. A decade is a long time to stick with one thing, so change can be good."

"Way to instill confidence in your girlfriend that this thing we're doing is long-term," Kira replied with a mock glare.

"Poor phrasing. In some matters, a decade would only be the beginning."

She ran her fingers through his hair. "It's hard to believe it's been a fourteen-year path to get here. Would you ever have guessed we'd end up in the Guard, if someone had asked you when we were teenagers, living on Valta?"

"Stars, no!" he laughed. "I think I was still planning to be a veterinarian back then."

"That's right! You had that master plan of working at the petting zoo at the Tribeca Nature Preserve."

"It would have been fun."

"Yeah, it would have." She shook her head. "And I would have been a Reader, entertaining tourists with mind-reading tricks. Ugh, but I would have hated every second of it."

"Life in the military suits you—helping people, going on adventurous missions, making a real difference in others' lives."

Kira gazed into his eyes. "As much as I enjoyed it before, something was always missing. Now, having you here, I have everything I ever wanted."

He brushed her hair back from her forehead. "No matter where you end up, I'll always be waiting to welcome you home."

She smiled. "When you put it like that, tackling those future unknowns doesn't sound so bad."

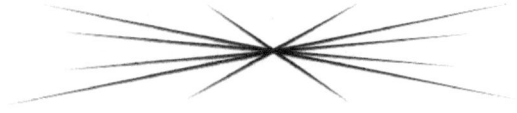

KIRA'S STORY WILL CONTINUE IN
THE TARAN EMPIRE SAGA!

For thousands of years, the Taran Empire has observed its lost colony of Earth from afar...

A new threat is on the horizon. In the aftermath of the Bakzen War, a spatial rift was left open at the edge of Taran space. Now, the Rift is growing, and an alien presence is trying to force its way through.

With the looming threat, it's time to bring Earth and other colony worlds into the Taran fold. Except, not everyone agrees the reunion is for the best. While the military prepares for battle against the transdimensional menace, the High Dynasties must try to unite their reborn Empire and prevent a civil war.

ALSO BY A.K. DUBOFF

Mindspace Series
Book 1: Infiltration
Book 2: Conspiracy
Book 3: Offensive
Book 4: Endgame

Cadicle Space Opera Series
Book 1: Rumors of War (Vol. 1-3)
Book 2: Web of Truth (Vol. 4)
Book 3: Crossroads of Fate (Vol. 5)
Book 4: Path of Justice (Vol. 6)
Book 5: Scions of Change (Vol. 7)

Dark Stars Trilogy
Book 1: Crystalline Space
Book 2: A Light in the Dark
Book 3: Masters of Fate

Troubled Space
Vol. 1: Brewing Trouble
Vol. 2: Stealing Trouble
Vol. 3: Making Trouble

AUTHOR'S NOTES

Thank you for reading this fourth book in the Mindspace series! I feel incredibly lucky to have such passionate, engaged readers.

Working on this project has been a great learning experience for me. It's not every day that an author has the opportunity to reimagine a story in a different universe. It was a unique challenge, and one I enjoyed. The Cadicle universe has been my 'happy place' since I was a pre-teen, so anything having to do with that world excites me.

When I wrote the original version of this series as the Uprise Saga, I had seven novels in my backlist, along with a handful of short stories and a couple of novellas. Now, that I have the Dark Stars trilogy as well as this revised four-book Mindspace series in the Cadicle universe, I feel like I'm well on my way to building an author brand.

I talked in the *Conspiracy* author notes about my attraction to the metaphysical, and the more I write, the more I realize I'd like for such superhuman abilities to be an ongoing theme in my stories. I want to try on different flavors of those elements, ranging from hard sci-fi to more fantasy-magic interpretations. I love the idea of pushing the boundaries for what it means to be human.

I hope to further develop this emerging brand. From a reader perspective, I want you to have confidence that you know what you'll get in my books. I've learned a *ton* about plotting and how to draw a reader in while writing Mindspace, and I look forward to bringing these new skills to future projects.

What's next for Kira?

When I started reimagining this series within the Cadicle umbrella, I had a decent sense of what was going to happen in the Cadicle sequel, Taran Empire Saga. Having an established covert ops character who specializes in dealing with politically tense situations would be an asset. So, as I was revisiting the central character for Mindspace, my plan was always for her to play a role in the big things to come for the Taran Empire.

Will Kira get more standalone books? I'm not sure yet, but I'm certainly open to the possibility. As it stands now, she'll certainly be a character in Taran Empire Saga, and we'll take it from there :-).

I hope you enjoyed the Jason cameo in this book and are excited to see how the changes throughout the Empire play out. Cadicle was very much a story of the people at the top of the power structure, and I hope Mindspace has given you a window into other aspects of life in the story universe.

Sincere thanks to Michael Anderle and Craig Martelle for giving me the opportunity to write the original version of this series and help launch my author career. It's was an incredible experience to see what's possible to achieve when you build a great relationship with your readers. I hope to embody this in my own career, and to one day be able to pay their mentorship forward to other authors.

As always, thank you to Nick, my husband, for always keeping my fed and happy—I would not have a better life partner or best friend. Thank you to Jen McDonnell for editing and to my beta readers and proofers—John, Jim, Kurt, Leo, Charlie, Troy, Eric, Curtis, Ron, Diane, Angel, and Nick—and the original LMBPN JIT team. I am so fortunate to work with such great people!

And thank *YOU* for reading and being a part of this author journey with me! I hope we can go on many more adventures together.

ABOUT THE AUTHOR

A.K. (Amy) DuBoff has always loved science fiction in all its forms—books, movies, shows and games. If it involves outer space, even better!

Now a full-time author, Amy can frequently be found traveling the world. When she's not writing, she enjoys wine tasting, binge-watching TV series, and playing epic strategy board games.

To learn more or connect, visit www.amyduboff.com.